Ten Grand

Seamus Heffernan

CROOKED
CAT

Discover us online:
www.crookedcatbooks.com

Join us on facebook:
www.facebook.com/crookedcat

Tweet a photo of yourself holding
this book to **@crookedcatbooks**
and something nice will happen.

To Chelsey

About the Author

Prior to his writing career, Seamus Heffernan worked in education, journalism, marketing and politics. Born in St. John's, Newfoundland, he has called several places home, including a lengthy stint in London, England. He currently resides in British Columbia, where he splits his time between Abbotsford, Mission and Vancouver.

Acknowledgements

I thank Lesley Breau and Alisa Mappes for their feedback on earlier drafts of this work.

I also thank my publishers, Laurence and Steph Patterson, for their support, patience and kind words as this manuscript came together.

Ten Grand

"Man is not what he thinks he is,
he is what he hides."

André Malraux

1

In my line of work, I usually ask the questions—I don't have to answer them. It's one of the perks of this job I like to remind people of. So I wouldn't normally agree to interviews, but as this had been a favour to a friend, I had found it hard to say no. The young man before me had been inquisitive, that was for sure, scribbling away at everything I said despite his smartphone recording our chat. I couldn't help but admire such diligence, even as it came across a bit self-serious. He had good posture and a knowing air, which I felt was perhaps unearned. I had answered his wide-ranging questions politely and fully, and he showed little interest in wrapping up anytime soon. He had a bit of moxie, sure, but he was also keen. I could respect that—but I made sure he noticed me taking a glance at my watch.

"How does someone get into this line of work?" he asked.

I shifted in my seat, giving my lapels a quick tug.

"Well, in my case…one thing just kind of followed another."

His brow knitted together a bit as he made more notes.

"Can you expand on that?" he asked.

"Sure. I used to do other jobs, and now I do this one."

He looked up, making a small circle in the air with his ballpoint.

"That's a bit cagey. But I can see it's personal," he said.

"It is, thank you. Why do you ask, by the way? Are you interested in working a job like this?"

He considered that.

"Hypothetically, sure."

"Well, what else do you want to know? About the job, I mean."

He mulled that over for a moment.

"What are the hours like?"

"Terrible."

"What's the money like?"

"Marginally better."

"Could you make more?"

"Sure."

"Why don't you, then?"

I paused to think it over.

"I could go work for a private security outfit or an insurance company. I've had a few offers, actually. That's where the majority of my cases come from."

"Why don't you?"

I laughed.

"Good question. I don't know. Guess I like the way my name looks on the front door."

"What kind of work do you do for those guys?"

"Background checks on potential employees and fraudulent injury claims, mostly. I also do missing persons work for people who have skipped out on their child support or other fiscal obligations."

"Do you like it?"

"Enough, yeah."

"Could you do other cases? Investigate other things?"

"Absolutely."

"Why don't you?"

"It's a long story."

"I have time."

I laughed again.

"I don't. So I'll keep it short: I don't want to. At least, not anymore."

He took his time writing something about that down. I couldn't tell if he was particularly intrigued or just buying some time before coming at me with another curveball.

"What's the economic outlook overall, for private investigators?" he asked.

"Pretty good. You can always make a few bucks on people's greed. Or their stupidity."

He took a breath, digging deep for another question. I

politely interjected.

"Last one," I said.

He didn't miss a beat.

"Would you recommend people go into this field?" he asked.

"You mean, become a PI?"

"Yeah."

I considered this before answering, but we were interrupted by a knock on the office door.

"Jeremy, that's 30 minutes. It's time to go. Leave Thaddeus alone and thank him for this time. He's a busy man."

"*Muuuuuum,*" young Bob Woodward here groaned. "It's for *school.*"

"Yeah, I think that should be good," I said, nodding thanks to Sarah, the mother in question. "You got enough, right?"

Clearly disappointed, he still nodded.

"You'll let me know when this is out?"

"Yeah, for sure. It's a big feature. About half a dozen of us are interviewing people with careers off the beaten path."

"That's pretty cool," I said. "Feel free to make stuff up to fill in the boring bits I gave you."

I smiled to let him know I was joking around. He didn't return it. Instead, he packed his bag and stuck out his hand.

"Thank you," he said, almost solemnly.

I stood, and we shook.

"No problem," I said.

Still gripping my hand, he asked, "Would you come to my class on career day?"

I began to laugh again and Sarah ushered him out.

"That's not a no," he said as she closed the door, facing me.

"Thank you for this," she said. "I figured since you used to be a teacher, you'd be OK to ask."

"Yeah, of course." Sarah had come to me about six months ago, suspecting her husband was stepping out. I referred her to someone I knew in town, someone good who would get it done fast and clean. She had been right, but more importantly she had been smart—instead of blowing her cool she held onto the photos, got into his phone and e-mails, found a good lawyer, and ate the now ex-hubby alive. When he moved out, she had come back to say thanks. We went out for dinner once, maybe twice.

"He's a good kid. Smart. Excellent attention to detail. He might be a good cop someday."

"Not a PI?" she asked, smiling coquettishly.

"Not glam enough," I said. "I could tell he was getting a bit disillusioned."

"I doubt that. You're a good storyteller."

"Well, then he will definitely be disappointed if you tell him that, 'cause most of my answers veered towards the monosyllabic."

"I doubt that too," she said. "In my experience, you're pretty verbose."

I sat back down.

"It's been good to see you," I said. I moved some paper around on my desk, trying to find a file.

"How have you been?" she asked.

I paused, to give the illusion that the answer would be the actual, thought-out truth.

"Not bad. Keeping busy. Work is OK."

"Good to hear," she said, pressing freshly lacquered lips together. "Well, I should get going"—she flicked her head towards the door—"before he figures out how to get into your hard drives or something."

"We'll be OK," I said, flipping open the laptop on my desk. There was an e-mail from an old friend, but it could wait. "Everything is right here, anyways. The one out in reception has long been wiped."

"Pretty quiet out there, lot of space," she said. "You going to get someone working out here, answer the phones or greet the clientele?"

I opened another file folder, looking for the casework on some brainless surveillance job whose paperwork I had let slip and needed to catch up on.

"I'm doing all right on my own," I replied. "I don't mind flying solo right now."

She dawdled for a moment.

"Jeremy's with his dad this weekend," she said.

"Mmhmm," I said, peeking under another stack. Success—there it was, tucked away.

I looked up. She was waiting. I hadn't twigged it.

"I'm working," I said. "Sorry."

It sounded a bit brusquer than I had intended. She nodded, a slight flush touching her cheeks.

"I'm sorry," I said, a bit more gently. I stood up again. "Really. I'm just trying to keep a lot of balls in the air here. My social life, such as it is, is a distant second."

"I get it." She tucked her clutch under her arm. "Say no more."

Like her son, she extended her hand. I took it, more gently than I had taken his.

"It was good to see you," she said. "Do take care, Thad."

"Someone once told me I would never be very good at that," I said as she stepped out. "But I'm trying."

2

I wasn't actually feeding Sarah a line—my weekend was well shot before she had even walked in. Friday night I had a tail job: A dad worried about his teenage daughter, who had been keeping some late hours and running with what he assumed was a bad crowd. A few hours looping around an admittedly dodgy pub in Brixton that was less than thorough about all its ID checking should put his mind at ease. Far as I could see, she was into playing board games, sitting too close to some black-jeaned, scruffy young guy and having a few sneaky shandies, but nothing too scandalous.

Satisfied, I had found another pub nearby, the kind without a jukebox or board games, seeing as the assortment of harmless elderly alcoholics huddled over their pork scratchings and racing forms would put up with neither. The bartender didn't even blink when all I asked for was a club soda, bless him.

My phone buzzed as I settled into my stool, taking in a Six Nations promo poster over the bar and a calendar, brittle and yellow, from 1986. They had still turned the month to February. A cartoon Cupid hovered over a silhouette of a couple.

"Grayle," I said.

"Hey. You free?"

Oh, that voice. Girly, but with just a hint of a long-ago whiskey rasp.

"For you? Most of the time," I said.

"You need some new material. We've only worked together a few months and I've heard that before."

"Get used to it," I said. "I only have about six good anecdotes, too, and you've heard four of 'em already."

"Let's make some more. Where are ya?"

I gave her my location. She wasn't too far from here—ten minutes or less, she said.

Those few months had gone by pretty quickly, truth be told. I had met Ayesha Gill, combat vet-turned-security consultant, when doing a big background check job for a corporate client. There had been a push on hirings, and they needed it done quickly and discreetly. Fortunately I was well placed for both. She was working a contract gig at the same time, some bodyguard work for visiting executives. She was amenable to taking on some more freelance work, and following the changes in my own business model, I needed someone with her skill set—and contacts.

Emboldened by my previous order, I had taken the liberty of ordering her a black coffee, gratefully accepted as she slid onto the stool next to me, even as she side-eyed my packet of salt and vinegar.

"So," I said. "What's the crack?"

"Could be a doozy." She tested the java. Still a bit hot. "This one's got all sorts of intrigue."

"Stop it. The suspense. You're killing me."

Ayesha smiled, that alabaster hook lighting up the bar's smooth wooden top and the brown bottles cluttering nearby.

"What?" I said, tired of waiting.

"So eager," she said, the smile shrinking only a bit. "So ready for adventure."

I sat back, shrugging.

"It's Friday night and I'm sitting in this place having a so-so bit of fizzy water and being judged for enjoying a bag of crisps," I said. "So maybe I've earned something exciting to distract me."

"I don't think you care what night it is," she said. "You've never said no when I've called."

"Keep calling. Next time I might be washing my hair. You'll have to find some other boy to spend time with."

"That's never been a problem," she said, and I was never more sure of someone else's truth.

So-so or not, I wrapped my hands around the ice-packed glass, content to let her have her moment and eventually get to the point.

"Wife, one kid - a son - living in West Brompton," she began. "Husband has been missing for a few days. Cops are all over it."

"Not surprising, considering the post code," I said. "What's the angle?"

"Money," she said. "What else?"

"Well, when men disappear it's usually over two things— money or sex."

"This one is the former," she said. "Trust me."

She slid an envelope across. I tapped my fingers against it, and my face must have looked less than enthralled.

"Thad," she said. "You're going to want to take this one."

I emptied the envelope and quickly scanned the contents.

Yannick Duclos, successful trader in the City. Disappeared three days ago, no warning, no explanation. Preliminary investigation showed he's squeaky clean with nothing to shade his exit—except for one thing that popped out as I skimmed the background.

"Not a cent?" I asked. "Guy's been working in the City for years, he pulls a runner and there's not a dime in any of his accounts?"

Ayesha nodded.

"Well, where is it now?"

"That's the thing," she said. "It's all gone. All of it. And so is he."

"Did he just clear 'em all out and just take off?"

"That's what the cops are trying to confirm, although apparently it's all legit. No sign of any real unusual activity with his bank. They're working the financial angle, they figure there has to be a trail somewhere. Wife is playing dumb, though. Working theory is, he's simply cut and run. The cops figure he's somehow hid a few bucks away and is likely headed to live a life of passable luxury in Thailand or some other place with nice beaches and a favourable exchange rate."

"Yeah, and they're probably right," I said. "Which is bad news."

"How's that?"

"Guy like that is going to be hard to find—'cause he's smart, has resources and obviously doesn't want to be found."

"Well, that's what I think, too. But the wife would like to broaden the scope of the investigation."

"If it's financial, the cops are the best bet."

"No kidding. I don't think he's going to turn up in a place like this. But she wants a second opinion. She thinks it's something else."

I returned to the envelope's contents. Flipped through—some press clippings, nominal stuff about the disappearance, little write up on the family. Some other bits and pieces—e-mails, mobile numbers and addresses. But the article had a pic of the family, all decked out for some big to-do. Mom and Dad, peacock-proud and sporting wide smiles.

The kid, though. Looked maybe 12, 13. His eyes were sad, sure, but there was more there. Hard to tell, but the son had the look of a kid who had seen a lot. He wasn't facing the camera, his eyes, little black angry puddles, veering off to the right.

"What does she think it is?" I asked.

"That's all I got. And even if I did know, I don't know if I'd tell ya. I think you're hooked now, but having to find that out from the wife would make it 100 percent, for sure."

I smiled. She got up.

"Tomorrow," she said. "Two o'clock. She said the kid will be out so you two can talk. House address and nearest tube station is all in there."

"I have another gig," I said. "Some denim place down Carnaby Street wanted someone to walk around, stake out the place—they thought someone on staff was ripping them off."

Her look was as close to pity as I would ever see from her.

"It pays well," I said, defensively.

"Christ, Thad. Are you serious?"

"Fine," I said, rolling my eyes for effect. "OK. I'll swing by."

She finished her tea.

"Please be gentle," she said. "Mrs. Duclos has been through a lot."

"You should've been with me when I worked infidelity

cases. I'm used to emotional wives. Husbands, too."

"This is different," Ayesha said. "This one actually wants her husband to come back."

3

Ayesha was right about one thing—I was intrigued. But I had my own family issues to contend with before any business the next day. Calls with my ex-wife weren't exactly causes of celebration, but that's not why I was sitting outside my favourite pie and pasty shop near Liverpool Station, about a ten-minute walk from my office, ruefully punching the international dialing code for Switzerland into my cell. I tend to view chores as things deserving of treats upon completion, and a fresh pork and apple seemed sufficient here.

Roxanne answered after one ring, efficient as ever.

"Thad."

"Rox."

"How are things?"

"Good. Keeping busy. You?"

"Same."

"Good to hear."

"Thank you."

"All caught up, then," I said, and couldn't help a smile I hoped didn't travel through the line.

It hadn't.

"Calls about child support aren't social occasions, you know," she said. "Even if you're always on time every month."

"Well, this call is different," I said. "That's why I wrote you. I have an idea."

"Do tell," she said, but I could tell she was at least curious —her natural acidity had dropped a bit.

"I know you and Reg want to get hitched," I said. Rox's current *amour*, Reginald Forsythe, was whatever a bigshot in a venture capital firm was. They had gone to Geneva for an opportunity that had, by all accounts, gone very well for his firm. "But if you do, it's no more alimony payments from yours truly."

"That's not the only issue," she said. "We've both been settling in here, building our new jobs—"

"It's OK," I said. "I'm not laying blame or giving you a hard time. But if we both want a total clean break, maybe we could compromise."

"How so?" More than a little curious now.

"How much would Amy's school be for, say, the next four years?" My daughter was enrolled—of course—in a prestigious private academy determined to produce the next generation of movers and shakers or, at the very least, well-heeled debutantes.

"Um," Rox did some mental math, perhaps slowed a bit by the natural shame all English people have of saying large money amounts out loud. "40 thousand pounds?"

"Jesus," I said. "Is she going to be an astronaut or something?"

"What?"

I ignored the question, plowing ahead. Explaining the joke would only give her the chance to remind me that I could be tiringly juvenile. "OK, so let's say I paid for that," I said. "Starting with ten grand now, and the rest divide across four years. That gets her out of high school without a dent in your finances."

"No more monthly payments?"

"Well, not officially, but I'd be happy to throw in when you guys needed it."

"We don't *need* it," she said. "We're doing pretty well. Also, she's your daughter, too, you know, so you should be chipping in."

"Exactly my point. I take responsibility for her education, you two can get married, and we all get to walk away clean."

"That's a lot of money," she said. "You got that just laying around?"

"Found an envelope in an old suit I hadn't worn in a while," I said. "Look, think it over. Talk to Reg. It's a good deal for you. "

"Good for you, too," she said. "I think it works out a little less than you would pay over the next five years."

I pulled the phone away for a second, covering the receiver with my hand so as to muffle the exasperated sigh I could not keep in.

"Until she turns 18 and then I don't have to anymore," I said. "Look, I'm not trying to nickel and dime you. Go do the figures, calculate it to the exact amount, I'll pay it. I just want to take care of this."

"What, her schooling?"

"Well, yes," I said. "And other stuff."

"Like what?"

"Like you."

This gave her pause.

"What do you mean?" she asked after a moment.

"I know you want get married," I said. "You told me a while back. This way, you get to do what you want."

"What do you want?"

"To take care of this crucial part of my daughter's life."

"Anything else?"

"That clean break."

Again, she waited before responding.

"Is that important to you?"

"It's important to *us*," I said. "Insofar as we can move on."

I could hear a muffled voice, and Rox shushing its owner.

"That Amy?" I asked.

"It is."

"Say hi."

"She's already gone."

"Well, later then," I said. "If it's not too much of a bother."

"I'll talk to Reggie about it," she said, as always expertly deflecting any of my sarcasm or jibes. Divorce doesn't change everything. "But I think we will have a deal."

"Good," I said, walking towards Warren's Bakery. The rich smell had been tugging at me for a bit and I figured I had now earned this appetite.

"What brought this on?" she asked. "Aside from the fact you're obviously doing well."

"What can I say? I'm a successful entrepreneur in this madcap thing we call late-stage capitalism, and I'm determined to wring every last dime from it and take care of my loved ones."

"'Ones'?" she asked. "I'm getting a little flushed here."

"Don't get too weak in the knees. You'll stretch out your good yoga pants."

This earned an honest-to-god laugh. A short one, but there it was.

"Thad," she said. "Thank you. Really. It's a good idea, and a generous one."

"You're welcome," I said. I had my hand on the handle. I could see one of the bakers inside. He recognized me and gave a wave. I pointed to the phone, eyes rolled. *Right there, fellas, just bankrolling my precocious child's future and my ex-wife is trying to say thank you without acknowledging in any way our shared past or her innate humanity. You know how it is.*

She picked up on my impatience.

"I'd best be going, too," she said. "I'll have Amy call you this weekend."

"Sure, thanks," I said. "Best to Reg, of course."

"Um. Really?"

"Nah," I said, and then we both laughed.

"Thanks again," she said. "This could be great for all of us."

"Well, as an enthusiastic former educator, it makes sense I would want to ensure this part of her life is well taken care of."

"Anything else?"

"I just want you to be happy," I lied. I pulled the door open —the bell above it jangled, signaling we were done. We said good-bye at the same moment, a brief verbal fumble that happens between bad timing and the weight of all the more unsaid. I cut off the call as she repeated herself.

4

Properly fed, I had made the half-mile trek from Earls Court station to meet with Ayesha's hot lead. The Duclos house was stucco-fronted and stood out, even in this posh West Brompton neighbourhood, as impressive. Mrs. Duclos—"Annie, please"—waved me in after a quick introduction. She was short and wiry, with jet-black hair tugged back into a loose ponytail, which bounced around the scoop collar of a faded t-shirt. She led me into the TV room, which overlooked a lush garden, spanning back about 50 feet. She grabbed the remote and muted what was on—an old zombie flick I recognized from a few late-night viewings back in my undergrad days.

"Sorry," she said, sitting and tucking her legs up under herself. "It was on and I got sucked in a bit."

"No worries,' I said, taking a seat and pulling loose my notepad. "I leave the radio on for company in my place all the time."

Her gaze lingered a bit on the screen. "Yannick is a big movie guy. He loves this stuff." Then, coming back to the moment: "You sure I can't get you anything?"

By way of answer, I clicked my pen into life.

"Best just to get started, I think," I said.

She nodded, squeezing her calves in a little closer.

"Ayesha gave me the basics," I began. "But I obviously have a lot more questions."

She nodded—audience was now granted.

"When was the last time you saw your husband?"

"Four nights ago. Around 8 o'clock. He had packed a bag and said he was away for a few days. Business. Somewhere in Salzburg. He said he was calling a taxi."

"Where's he work?"

"Bergman Hapsburg. Financial advisers, brokers, that sort

of thing."

"You don't hear from him, so you call his office and I'm assuming no one has any idea where he is, and there was no business trip?"

She nodded.

"I assume the cops have been through his laptop, belongings, everything?"

"Yes."

"What have they told you?"

"They've made some rumblings about enemies, which is almost laughable," she said. "They've also inquired as to his mental health, which I imagine is standard in these sorts of things."

"It is. Was he depressed?"

"No more than most middle-aged, middle-class men."

"But no less?"

Rather than answer, she grabbed the remote and turned the TV off. Some clients like a little back-and-forth. Annie Duclos was not going to be one of them.

"What's the last you heard from them?" I asked.

"They're going through what they have termed the usual missing person protocols, but they also have forensic accountants tearing our paper lives apart."

"Why don't you think that's enough? The police investigation, I mean."

"I don't understand the question."

I looked up from my notepad, careful to keep my face neutral.

"Why are you considering hiring outside help?" I asked. "Why am I here?"

"To supplement the investigation. I thought that would be obvious."

I stood and straightened the cuffs of my shirt before beginning to wander to the back door.

"Nice yard," I said, peering out from under my hand. "Is that a shed?"

"Home office, actually." She stayed on her couch, giving her surroundings a disparaging glance. "We haven't had any work done to this place in ages."

"The office, yours or his?"

"His."

I stepped towards the mantle.

"Just the one child?" I asked, nodding towards a picture.

She nodded.

"Where is he now?"

"Aiden is at, uh"—she struggled to remember the name and her nose scrunched for a second as she dug deep, before finally—"I think it's called Gosh."

I glanced up.

"The comic shop?"

She nodded again.

"I know it," I said. "Great Russell, near the museum."

"Not anymore. Moved to Soho a couple years back."

"Hunh. I haven't been for a while. My daughter loves that place, though."

"Perhaps they've crossed paths there," she said.

I continued to inspect the mantle and its accompanying family arcana. "Not likely," I murmured.

"Why not?"

I gave her a look, quick but direct. She looked away. Message received. My own fault, really. It just kind of came out, a personal detail, when kids and comic books were broached.

"How is he holding up with all this?" I asked.

"He's OK. Hanging in there."

"How old?"

"13."

"Tough age," I mused.

"And not a tough kid," she added.

I smiled a little at that, not unkindly. I sat back down.

"Is there something wrong?" she asked. "I'd have thought you'd want to get moving on this quickly."

"Sure," I said. "But you still haven't answered my question."

Her lips, flat until that point, moved up a bit, but it was not a happy smile.

"Very good, Mr. Grayle," she said.

I shrugged. "So I'll ask again: why am I here?"

She sighed and stepped away to the kitchen, she returned with two Cokes, handing me one as she popped the tab on her own. I laid my can down, unopened, on a nearby coaster.

"It's possible that I have not been completely forthright with the police," she finally said as she resumed her perch on the couch.

"I would advise against holding back from them," I said.

She looked bemused.

"You don't seem surprised," she said.

"I'm not easily excitable. Look, Mrs. Duclos—"

"Annie," she corrected.

"Annie," I continued. "The police are actually quite good at this. Lots of people try to outsmart them and end up finding out they weren't as clever as they thought they were. These cops are going to rip your husband's life apart and find out pretty much everything about him, both what's on paper and what's not. So, if I were you, I'd save myself a lot of money and not hire me. I'd also save myself a lot of hassle and not get jammed up on a withholding evidence charge."

"Funny, I had imagined that someone in your line of work would hold the police in a bit more…disdain."

"Get to know me a bit. I like everyone."

"Be that as it may," she said. "I'd still like to hire you."

"Let's hear the why, please. I imagine it has something to do with him taking off without a word and, I'm guessing, leaving you high and dry, bank-wise."

"Your sources are very good, as are your instincts. I imagine that's a big part of the reason you were recommended to me."

"Well, I don't really have any hobbies, so I've had more energy to dedicate to my career. It's finally paying off."

She got up and drifted towards the mantle. I caught her eyes flicking towards the family photos. She was working up to spilling it, but clearly needed a bit of inspiration.

"My husband, Yannick, is a shrewd man. He spent years handling money for a wide range of clients, some of whom were astonishingly wealthy. There were the standard tax havens and trusts, of course, but also some money that had to be…cleaned up a bit. He charged a lot more for that."

"I can imagine."

If she felt anything resembling shame, she was already coming across as someone who would go to the grave before admitting it.

"And he was also a shrewd investor himself," she continued. "He had been using clients' money to buy up large shares in companies, then dumping the stock for quick profit and moving the original money back."

"You think someone found out? Maybe a client? That's why he's cut and run?"

She shook her head.

"His name isn't on anything. And the money is in a Swiss account."

"How much are we talking about? This, well, shadow money?"

She picked at a hangnail. Sighed.

"About four million pounds," she said.

Jesus.

"And it's still there?" I asked, trying hard to match her stony vibe.

"Yes."

"Wait. Hang on. So, how much money do *you* have?"

She pulled her phone from her pocket, opened her banking app and held it out.

Under CHEQUING: It said £348.65.

Under SAVINGS: £14.32.

"Well," I said. "You're gonna have to dip into that Swiss account."

"That is… complicated."

"How so?"

"Only my husband has the account details," she said. "He didn't even write them down. Too risky, he said. He has it all memorized."

"Seriously?"

"He was an avid fan of puzzles and games," she said, and

23

her tone suggested that even in these circumstances she still found her husband's hobbies trying. "So, as you can see, there is a certain urgency to finding him."

"No kidding. You have anyone who can help you out?"

She shook her head.

"All on our own," she said. "It's quite serious. We could lose the house. My son will have to leave his school."

She didn't sound sad or even bitter. I was starting to think Mrs. Duclos would be all right even without four million, but that would be in the long term. The short term, well—that is why somebody like me is in a place like this.

"You're sure no one knew about this?" I asked. "You seem pretty confident that he is alive and on the run, and not the more obvious answer."

"You mean, that he is dead?"

I nodded.

"My husband was preternaturally boring," she said. "He was far too careful to have enemies. But he did have… moods."

"Define 'moods.'"

"This isn't the first time he's done this," she said. "But it is the first time he has been gone so long."

"You mean, just disappear?"

"Yes," she said. "Just …gone."

We fell into a silence, one I let hang for a bit.

"OK, I'm interested," I finally said.

"I'm hoping we can negotiate some form of payment plan."

"Yeah, I have an idea about that. That four million, how much of it is legit? That Yannick earned and not, uh…"

"Stole?"

"Well, I was going to try and phrase it a bit more diplomatically, but sure: Stole."

She considered for a few seconds.

"Probably a third."

"Your guy works at that level of finance for that long and only managed to hold onto that much?"

She looked at me with a mix of sadness and amusement, like a parent trying to explain something painfully obvious to a doltish child.

"Life is expensive, Mr. Grayle. Sometimes, it's as simple as that."

"*Your* lives, you mean."

"Those are the only lives I can worry about right now."

I nodded, mulling it over.

"All right. If I take this case my job will be to find your husband before the cops do, and get you access to that money so you can keep your nice house and keep your kid in a nice school. Correct?"

She nodded.

"OK. Assuming I meet those expectations, what's the offer?"

Unsurprisingly, but still to her credit, she didn't even blink. No hesitation whatsoever.

"The offer is 25 percent. I will sign over a quarter of whatever is in that account to you."

"So… a million pounds?" I asked.

"Yes." Still, that voice. Flat, giving away nothing. "Roughly. One million pounds sterling."

I considered this. The truth is, there were other options. I could offer an actual payment plan, attempt to squeeze out a sizable retainer up front—I take credit cards—or simply say no. Walk away. Saying "yes" meant I was running a big risk— I could put in a lot of work here and still end up with nothing if her husband managed to stay hidden.

Still, though, Ayesha had been right. I *was* intrigued. If nothing else, it would beat insurance scam tail jobs and following underage drinking teenagers for a while.

Those were the options. Even as I opened my mouth, I was unsure what I would say.

"All right," I said, maybe surprising myself a little. "You have a deal."

"Excellent," she said. She stepped towards me and extended her hand. "We can have the papers drawn up immediately."

I looked at the hand, awaiting mine.

"No offense, but how are we going to write this as a legally binding contract?" I asked.

She laughed.

"My husband manipulated, cajoled and ultimately stole millions and no one knew anything about it," she said. "I can promise there will be a way to make sure you get your money."

"Promises are something kids make to each other on playgrounds," I said.

"Would you prefer to pinky swear, then?"

She smiled a bit then, a real one. There was apparently a little velvet swathing Mrs. Duclos' steel.

"Nah," I said. "What the hell. Without trust, what else is there?"

She held that smile.

I shook her hand.

5

Detective Inspector Ian Calloway emerged, all smiles, from the side entrance of St. James and St. John Church in Ealing. It was late—shortly after 9 p.m.—but he showed little sign of tiredness or any Sunday-before-Monday grumpiness. Calloway's mood had improved immensely in his last year of work with Professional Standards. I can only assume that ferreting out crooked coppers and alienating most of the rest of the force helped maintain his sunny disposition.

"Evening," he greeted me, as we fell into step.

"Hey," I said. "How was the meeting?"

"Pretty good, yeah," he said. "I make it pretty much every week. There's actually one a bit closer to mine but I like these church basements."

"How's that?"

"I don't know," he shrugged. "Better coffee? The usual self-reproach that comes with passing by religious iconography? Keeps one honest, you have to admit."

"I was raised Catholic. I've had enough self-loathing, thanks."

"You lot do make a fuss about that," he said. "Much ado about nothing, I'd wager."

"I come by it honestly enough. More than a few crucifixes in my house growing up. And my mom used to keep a card of St. Jude as a bookmark. Patron saint of lost causes."

"Among other things, yes."

"You never struck me as a theologian, DI."

"I'm not. More just intrigued by the history and rituals. Besides, your Catholicism and my Anglicanism are pretty much first cousins on the Christianity family tree."

"My grandmother would have called you out on that," I said. "Imagine, me talking to a common Protestant.

Scandalous."

"Probably for the best she doesn't know how you pay your bills as an alleged grown-up, then. On that topic: Do you have it?"

I made a bit of a show of sighing before reaching into my coat and producing his fee: A copy of the opera *Die Tote Stadt* by Erich Wolfgang Korngold.

His eyes narrowed before accepting the prize.

"What year is the recording?"

"1975," I said. "Live in Munich."

Satisfied, he accepted the case and turned it over in his hands, his smile widening.

"You could always just get this stuff yourself," I said.

"What's the fun in that?" he said, and I could actually see his point. For Calloway, this was probably the same as eating someone else's French fry or someone else making you a sandwich: It was just better, somehow.

"You know Korngold was actually two people?" I said.

He rolled his eyes. "Look who learned to use a bit of Google."

"Hey man, I'm trying to have something for us to make small talk about. An interest in others' passions is a good start."

"Different time and different place, maybe. But I have five minutes here. So: What do you need?"

"The Duclos thing, missing rich dude I told ya about," I said. "Who's leading the investigation on your guys' side?"

Calloway was still smiling, but it now had a bit of curiosity to it.

"The wife bringing you in? For real?"

"Like she said: to supplement the investigation," I said. "I just spent the last day going through his very sparse address book and non-existent social media."

"Boring people make for boring cases."

"No kidding," I said. "So, who's running the case on your end?"

"Detective Inspector Felicity Dunsmore," he said. "Bit of an up-and-comer in the Missing Persons Unit."

"What's she like?"

"What I've heard is same as what I've seen when dealing with her. She's good police. Sharp, and she follows through. She knows MP is not the best place, ambition-wise. I reckon she's gunning for a big case or two to get a chance to move on."

"Anything else?"

"What is this, speed date by proxy?"

"C'mon."

"By reputation, she's a stickler for detail," he said. "So she's not going to be thrilled you're involved."

"I honestly don't know if you're complimenting me or not."

"I'm sure you do."

"Oh, stop. I hate it when we fight."

We were at Calloway's car, a non-descript but still quite decent Volvo.

"New wheels?"

"Gotta treat yourself every now and then," he said. He punched a text into his phone, and my inner jacket trembled.

"That's her number," he said. "Call her, as a courtesy. Introduce yourself. Tell her everything she already knows."

"Like what?"

"You know. I'm just here to help, I'll stay out of your way, let's share info, we're all on the same side. *Blah blah blah*, as you Yanks might say, right? But make sure she feels like she's the one definitely in charge."

"So sensitive," I said. "Why would I do that?"

"Because she is, you idiot." He opened the car door and slid in, but left it open.

"How's everything else?" he asked.

I shrugged. "Not bad. Keeping busy."

He held my gaze for a moment.

"I'm good," I said. "Sober, mate. Scout's honour."

"Keep it that way," he said. "The wife, Mrs. Duclos. She's broke, right, her and the kids? How are you getting paid?"

"I don't until the end of the job," I said, skipping over the possible illegality of the arrangement.

He shook his head. "That's risky. Bordering on stupid. You

know as well as I do most missing persons who are found, it's within 24 hours. Something like this, where the guy obviously has time, resources and no known enemies? He wants to be gone."

"Maybe," I said. "Or maybe he's just buying himself time."

"For what?"

"Jesus, Calloway," I said. "I don't know yet. That's why guys like us have a job."

He bristled at that a bit.

"I have a job because I wanted to serve the people of London and the United Kingdom and do so by being part of one of the most storied law enforcement agencies in history," he said. "You have a job because, I don't know, you read too many trashy novels as a kid. Watched a few episodes of *Cracker* and thought, oh that looks like fun, but I'll skip all the boring parts of becoming a cop and pretend taking photos of cheating husbands is the same thing."

"We haven't caught up in a while," I said. "I don't do that stuff anymore."

"Cheating husbands, missing husbands—whatever. You still answer to a client."

"We all answer to someone."

"Not really," he said. He slid the CD into the car's player. "Like you said, we haven't caught up in a while. I police *other* police. They answer to me, for the most part."

I rolled my eyes. He turned up the volume.

"Night," he said. "Thanks for the disc. Try not to spend that retainer in one place, yeah?"

Calloway could, I was learning, always be counted on to put me in what he thought was my place. Still, he was a decent enough guy. And my only friend at Scotland Yard. He extended his hand, and I took it.

"The TV show was *Crime Story,* actually," I said. "My mom let me stay up late Fridays to watch. You were close, though."

"You didn't need a TV show," he said as he started to pull away from the curb. "Yours is a vivid enough imagination, Grayle. Take care."

6

I arrived at St. Ann's Academy the next morning, bright and early, amazed as always at both the chipper energy and quiet air of entitlement uniformed kids could exude. I already felt tired facing it as I took the entrance steps two at a time, hoping the head had coffee in his office.

Headmaster Benedict Montrose was younger than I had imagined, with blonde hair carefully slicked back and parted neatly to the side. Instead of a sweater vest or tweed jacket, he paired a crisp white Oxford shirt and repp tie. His sleeves were even rolled up. I felt self-conscious of my navy suit as he guided me to a soft chair in front of his desk—it's not often you get to the principal's office and feel overdressed.

"Tea?" he asked. Damn it. I shook my head and he settled in, leaning forward, his pink skin looking clean and relatively line-free as the morning sun split the venetians.

"So," he said. "I understand you'd like to talk about the Duclos boy?"

"Yes," I said, pulling my notebook loose and fiddling with my visitor lanyard. It had caught on the inside of my suit jacket. "I'm sure the mother has contacted you, or otherwise I wouldn't have even gotten through the door."

He nodded, but waited for me to start.

"Aiden Duclos," I said. "How has he been coping?"

Montrose considered before answering.

"As well as could be expected. Obviously, there has been some unfortunate teasing from other boys."

"What are his friends like?"

"He struggles in that area."

"Clubs, sports, activities…?"

Montrose shook his head.

"Aiden is gifted academically, and a quiet and polite

31

enough child to avoid making any waves or drawing undue attention, either from staff or his peers. He is making his way through here, but we would like to see him do a bit more than, well…"

"Glide?" I asked. Montrose shrugged.

"This is a school, of course, and our focus is on education. But part of that education is preparing these boys to be well-rounded young men when they face the world."

"Looks to me a lot of these boys won't be facing the world when they get out of here, so much as running it," I said.

"You'd be surprised," Montrose countered. "Wealth and privilege are real things, to be sure, but many of these boys have struggles and demons just as well as anyone else."

"Let me guess: you also have a scholarship for a deserving underprivileged kid from, say, Hackney, preferably from a visible minority family."

Montrose didn't respond right away, waiting just long enough for the silence to become briefly awkward.

"You're cynical enough to be a detective, I'll give you that," Montrose finally said.

I looked down at my notes, and cleared my throat.

"Sorry. Occupational strain, I suppose. You see a lot."

Montrose shooed my apology away.

"Not a second thought, please, Mr. Grayle. I want to help as best as I can. Ask away."

"Well, you've said he's not Captain Popularity," I said. "But what's he like, you know, as a kid? What are his interests?"

Montrose pulled a yellow folder from a pile of them and dropped it in the centre. He opened it.

"Moody, struggles to participate in class, shies away from direct questions even though he clearly knows the answers. Excels in group work, likely because he takes on all the work rather than suffer at the hands of other students' limitations or laziness. Outstanding grades across the board, with a special affinity for English Lit. Which bring me to this…"

He slid a small stack of stapled papers across to me, a short story written by Aiden. I flipped through it. It featured a boy, an invisible monster that sets up shop at the kitchen table for meal-time, and that monster's gruesome end via the boy's wits, cunning and a very large knife.

"Not bad," I said. "Pretty solid start, and it has a clear beginning, middle and end."

Montrose allowed himself a small smile.

"That aside," he said, "The imagery was deemed a bit strong by his teacher. We asked Aiden to speak to the school counselor."

"What, for a bit of gore? He's a kid. They love this stuff."

"Normally, I'd agree with you. But here we wanted to make sure there was nothing else going on with the boy. As I said, he is a moody child."

"What'd the counselor say?"

"Without too many specifics, he was satisfied Aiden was not a killer, of monsters or otherwise."

"That's good to know," I said, flipping the notebook closed. "Can I speak to him?"

"Mrs. Duclos said you would want to, and we have arranged for you to have some time at recess," Montrose said, glancing at the clock. "Which will be in a few minutes. We've asked him to come here. You may use this office."

"Is it all right if I talk to him alone?"

"Of course," Montrose said, standing. He pulled a windbreaker, branded with the school's crest, off a hook. "You can use my office, if you'd like. I like to do a quick walk through the school grounds at the breaks, make sure everything is well within normal levels of anarchy and degradation."

"There's a theory about that in criminology," I said. "That visual deterrence of law enforcement is most effective when it's carried out by police on the ground, interacting with civilians, cracking down on minor offenses."

"Really? Interesting," Montrose said, zipping up. I wasn't sure if he was just being polite, but for some reason I wanted him to know I was at least a little bit smart.

"Yeah, it argues that problems start when we let the little stuff slide," I continued. "It allows escalation to bigger crimes."

"I can see that working at a school level," Montrose said, nodding. "Not sure about in major urban areas, though. Tell me, were you a police officer before this?"

I laughed. "No. Um, I was a teacher, actually. Just for a little while, though."

Montrose's turn to laugh a bit. "Well, then I'm sure you'll be great with Aiden. One more thing, if I may, Mr. Grayle. I'm curious."

"Shoot."

"In your example: Why does the crime necessarily escalate?"

"In theory? It's the same as life," I said. "When you don't take care of the small stuff, the big stuff comes back to bite you in the ass."

7

Montrose left me to my own devices as he took to patrolling what passed for the rough and tumble outside, telling me Aiden would be along shortly. I took the opportunity to check out his bookcase and return a missed call from Ayesha.

"So, thinking about going back to your old job?" she asked.

"Not a chance," I replied. "Not here at least. These kids don't need somebody like me."

"Is that your self-congratulatory way of saying you don't need them?"

"Six of one, half dozen of another," I replied. Montrose had, of course, a few classics of literature lining his wall, including some James Joyce and Dickens, but also some heavy history texts—ranging from Howard Zinn to Simon Montefiore. A lot of his books, though, were on child psychology, covering issues like conflict resolution and the effects of trauma. I was beginning to think that the headmaster might be that rarest of breeds in elite education—a genuine humanitarian. "What's up?"

"I need some work, was thinking you might have a few leads."

"You usually bring me work," I said.

"I'm diversifying. You working on anything cool?"

"I might be," I said. "So far, so good. I'll keep you posted, though."

"Do that. I'm getting stir crazy."

"Didn't that other bodyguard gig just wrap up, like, a week ago?"

"I don't deal well with dead time," she said. "I've got to keep moving. Like a shark."

"That shark thing's a myth."

"Fine. A woman's gotta eat, then. Sharks still eat, right?"

There was a knock at the door, two meek taps.

"That's the rumour, but you're not going hungry yet," I said, wrapping the call. "Like I said, I'll get back to ya when I need ya."

I opened the door. Aiden Duclos, all five feet and maybe 90 pounds of him, looked up from under the flop of blonde hair shrouding his eyes.

"Hi," I said. "I'm Thad."

"Hey." He made to step inside, but I held up my hand.

"Nah, not here. Let's go for a walk."

He shrugged and fell into step beside me as I took my time walking down the hall. Students milled at lockers, swapping snacks and homework. Music played from too-loud earbuds that were passed around. I could hear shouts and the occasional shriek outside. I stopped at a water fountain.

"Mom says you're helping to find my dad," Aiden said.

"I am, yes," I said, wiping my chin. "But I want to ask you a few questions, if that's all right."

"Sure, but I already talked to the cops."

"Do you watch TV?" I asked.

He nodded.

"Well, this is the part of the programme where a guy like me says, 'I'm not the cops.'"

He smiled at that a bit.

"So, you're like a bounty hunter?" he asked.

"Nah, nothing that cool. I'm a private investigator. People hire me to help out with stuff the cops won't, or might be too busy to get around to."

"Are the cops not trying to find my dad?"

"Oh no, believe me, they are looking for him very hard. Your mom thinks I might get him first, though. But to get started I gotta check in with people who know your dad. That's why you're stuck talking to me for a few minutes."

We hit the end of the hall. The band room was to our left, and through the open door I could see it was empty. I led him in and closed the door partway. We sat in the front row. Violin cases were at our feet. I took out my notebook.

"When'd you last see your father, Aiden?"

"That night. He came home from work. He had dinner with us. I went to bed around eleven. He was gone in the morning and didn't come back that night."

"Did you go straight to sleep?"

"No, I stayed up and watched stuff on YouTube."

"What kind of stuff?"

"Chappelle show clips. Some pimple popping vids. And then a guided meditation."

"You have trouble sleeping?"

He shrugged.

"How late were you up?

"Like, 2 a.m.," he said. He looked at my notebook with a little curiosity and a little boredom. "The cops know all this, you know."

"Well, they haven't decided how much they want to share just yet. So by two a.m., nothing weird? No sounds? No fighting between your parents?"

He shook his head.

"How was your dad at home?"

He regarded me, quizzically. "What do you mean?"

"You know, was he a nice guy, let you pick the movies to watch, brought home pizza every Friday? Or was he a shouter, did he ever hurt you or your mom, did he drink too much, you know—that kind of thing."

Aiden sat very quietly for a few seconds.

"My dad was OK," he finally said.

"Just OK?"

"He worked a lot. And he was moody a lot. And he'd forget stuff sometimes. Mom said he was distracted. Had a lot on his mind."

I considered this.

"Aiden, did your dad ever say anything about wanting to disappear or run away? Did you ever think he was maybe too stressed out to deal with stuff?"

"I don't know," he said. "He seemed pretty normal. Like, for an adult."

"How's your mom been since he left?"

He shrugged again.

"Sad, I guess. But she's trying to keep busy. Lot of reading, lot of time online."

He fidgeted a bit.

"Anything else?" I asked, gently. "Anything you say is between us, and it could be useful."

"I found a few empty wine bottles behind the recycling," he said. "I guess she waits until I'm asleep."

"Your mom drink a lot normally?"

"No."

"Where are your mom's friends?"

He snorted.

"Dad was Mum's friend, and they weren't even really friends," he said. "I don't think she knows a lot of people."

"Your dad has friends?"

"I guess. But if he did, they're not coming around."

We sat in silence for a minute. He played with the sheet music in front of him, dog-earing a corner then methodically smoothing it back into place.

"Is my dad dead?" he asked.

I tapped my notebook against my leg.

"I don't know," I said. "But I don't think so."

"Do you find a lot of missing people?"

"Just one, so far," I said. "And I didn't really find her. But this is different."

"How come?"

"Your dad looks like he is a pretty smart guy. And smart guys are good at staying out of trouble. That alone tells me he might just be hiding or taking some time for himself."

"Must be nice," Aiden said, getting back to the paper. "Pull a runner whenever you fancy it."

I didn't have an answer for that. Time to flip the switch.

"What was with that story you wrote for English, the monster one?" I asked.

His head whipped around, the hair snapping a bit.

"How'd you see that?"

"I do my research. Look, relax. I'm not ragging on it. You had some good stuff there."

He scowled, and his face wore the lines well—as if well-practiced.

"It was just a story," he said. "It's no big deal."

"I know that," I said. "But you gotta play by the rules."

"What do you mean?"

"You can't give them a reason to label you or worry about you. Give them the platitudes. Make it easy for them, and save your stuff for yourself."

"I guess… I don't know. It just came out when I was writing it."

"I get it," I said. "Now you know, though."

The bell rang. He stood.

"Nice to meet you, Aiden," I said, rising as well. "Thank you for your help."

He nodded.

"Did you finish the story?" he asked.

I shook my head.

"The only way to kill the monster is you have to kill the house," he said. "Destroy it. It's what gives the thing its power —the house."

"Oh yeah?" I asked, pulling my phone out and checking my messages. Another text from my old friend. I would have to make the time, I realized. "How do you do that?"

The pause was long. I realized Aiden was waiting for me to look up from my mobile.

"You burn it," he said. "To the ground. With everyone and everything still inside."

We were still standing there, holding each other's gaze, barely noticing when the violinists arrived.

8

Taylor Brock, soul-calloused divorce lawyer and a former drinking buddy of mine from way back, had been peppering my phone and e-mail with vague yet insistent demands that we meet. After my visit to St. Ann's I finally had a free hour, so we hastily arranged to connect in our usual spot near St. Paul's tube station. It was a small café where we often sat outside and watched the world go by: Me enjoying the hustle and bustle, he attempting to smile and hold eye contact with any woman who had the bad luck to glance up as she passed. His incorrigibility in this regard was well-documented: he was now on his third marriage, which if not yet on the rocks was getting dangerously close to the shoreline. I had assumed this is what he wanted to consult about. Immediately after sitting down, though, I realized I had gotten it wrong.

"Hey," I said. His eyes were sunk deep and ringed with purple. He had a day or two's worth of stubble on his jaw and a smile that was thinner than foolscap. His head carried a battered Mariners cap, faded blue and well-creased, a gift from me a long time ago. Whatever it was, it couldn't be the wife. I had never seen him this upset about a woman.

"All right?" he asked. I nodded.

He slid a paper cup, still steaming, across the table to me.

"I got here a few minutes ago," he said. "I know what you like."

I took a tentative sip, waiting for him to work up to the point.

"How is it?" he asked. "Too hot?"

I slid the coffee back a bit, shaking my head. Seeing him like this, I was in no mood for delay tactics.

"Brock. C'mon. What's going on?"

He linked his fingers and pushed his arm out so his palms

40

faced me, then brought them to his face, which he rubbed, hard.

"Thad," he said. "Jesus, man. I'm in trouble."

"You need a meeting?" I asked. Much like me, Brock had a past with alcohol that involved a lot of apologies. His had also included twelve steps and one or two sponsors.

He shook his head, hard.

"Not that kind of trouble," he said, flashing that anorexic grin again. "Worse, if you can believe it."

"Well, we've been friends for a long time, so I'm well prepared."

He looked up at me from under his cap's bill. I could see his eyes were welling up. It was a rare enough sight I felt my own breathing snag for a second.

"Brock," I said, a bit softer. "What's going on?"

"I, uh," he started. Then stopped. Deep breath. I gave him a small nod of encouragement.

"I owe a lot of money," he finally said.

"How much?"

"About eight thousand."

"OK. Not great, but not, you know, catastrophic."

He laughed, a weak little yelp.

"It is to these guys."

"You want to tell me how you got in this hole and who's waiting for their money?"

He drank, deeply, from his own coffee.

"I was broke. I owe child support on one marriage, two sets of alimony and a third coming up. I made a few bets."

"Shit's sake, Brock."

He held up his hand.

"Shut up. Let's just assume I know that this was all very stupid and so I don't need your further admonishment, OK?"

I nodded. "What'd you get into?"

"Horses, mostly. Some sports. It got out of hand. I couldn't cover it, so I went to a guy." He pressed his face into the makeshift cradle of his hands. "Anyhow. I'm behind. Way behind."

"How long you got?"

41

"A week."

"What do you have?"

"About two thousand."

"Can't you borrow the rest? Legitimately?"

He laughed again.

"Believe me, the banks and I, we aren't playing nice lately. I mentioned the child support and alimonies, right?"

I let some air escape through pursed lips. I had wired Rox the money I promised, and despite business being OK, it had cleaned out most of my savings. I had taken a big hit when I got out of the cheating spouse game, truth be told.

"It's not a great time right now," I said, finally.

He nodded. He pulled the cap lower against his eyes.

"What happens in a week?"

"What do you think?" he asks. "Beatings will continue until morale improves, isn't it?"

He gave a quick look about, then pulled his shirt up. His right side sported a purple welt in the shape of a ragged half-moon. I met his eyes. They were a little wet again.

I clenched and unclenched my jaw. I wondered if he could see.

"I could maybe see about getting some cash coming in," I said after a moment. "Plus, I have a little bit socked away."

"Yeah?"

"Could do, yeah. Plus, I'm working something interesting. If it breaks fast, it could be helpful here."

"What's the case?"

"Um. Well." I drank from my own cup. Put it down. Fiddled with my napkin.

"Sorry," he said, getting the message.

"Can't really talk about it," I said. I felt a bit badly. "Even the generalities, especially with you... now compromised. I mean, with the guys you're into for this. You understand, right?"

"Yeah, yeah. I get it."

We sat in silence for a minute. I did some mental math, trying to remember when the school cheque would clear, what I had left in savings, and how much my own bank manager liked me.

"Next Saturday," I said. "I can have some money for you by then."

"Well, that's the thing."

I felt my eyelids narrowing.

"What's the thing?" I asked.

"It's actually this Wednesday. I meant a week, like, generally."

I turned away. One thing about us addicts, we are fast and loose with the truth and good at sidestepping the minor inconveniences of other people's lives.

"Sorry," he said.

"Wednesday," I repeated. "As in, two days?"

"Yeah."

"Could you even, I don't know, pretend to be fussed about this?"

He rolled his shoulders. Not so much a shrug as an admission. No, not that—an acceptance.

"I think it's pretty clear the stakes," he said. "I've made my peace with it."

"If they kill you, they don't get their money."

"They won't kill me," he said, watching a blonde saunter by and not bothering being subtle about it. "But they will, uh, drag it out quite a bit. And get the money, eventually. How much of me is left, well, that'll be the issue."

I watched the back of the woman's head, golden ponytail bobbing as she worked her way down towards Cheapside. Maybe out to do a spot of shopping, or grab a bite with some friends. The normal, everyday stuff.

"Who do you owe the money to?" I asked.

"Why is that important?"

"Because I know a few people and I might be able to ask around, buy you a few days. Buy us a few days, 'cause I don't think I can be ready, either."

He considered this. I reached into my jacket and slid over my notebook.

"Name and address," I said. "That's all I need."

He scribbled it down and pushed it back.

43

"That it?" he asked.

I nodded, standing.

"I'll message ya when I have more info. Until then, keep a low profile."

"Yeah, I know."

"Stay away from the track. And the pubs. And, well, anywhere a reprobate like you would have any fun, really."

"Shut up, Thad," he said again. But his smile was a bit fuller.

I turned, about to walk away.

"You never asked me to say thank you," he said. "Just as well. I wouldn't know how."

"That's all right," I said, stopping and turning back a bit. "You threw a lot of snoop work my way back in days of yore. And you pulled me out of one or two scrapes. We're cool."

He kept the smile on, but we both knew it: That stuff was all small time compared to this.

"We're cool," I said again. "We're mates."

"We're mates?"

I was genuinely taken aback. "Of course we are," I said.

"Well. OK. I owe ya one."

"Well, no," I said, re-buttoning my jacket. "You'll owe me six grand, but we can sort that out after this is over."

He waved to our waitress, signaling for the check.

"I got your coffee," he said. He tweaked he bill of his cap one last time. "Least I can do, right?

9

Even though it had been over a year since I had stopped into the Bells Pub in the East End, as I pulled out a stool at the bar the governor there recognized me quickly—if a bit begrudgingly.

"Grayle," Shane Bowering said, shooing away the other barman and making his way down to re-explore our acquaintance. "Well, well. What's going on, detective man?"

Bowering had helped me out on another case, after I first threatened him and then bribed him. Obviously, I'm not great at making friends, but we had left it in an OK place. Still, we didn't send each other Christmas cards or anything. I extended my hand as a declaration of peaceful intent. Bowering accepted it, with only the polite amount of bemusement and disdain.

"Diet Coke?" he asked.

"You do remember your punters," I said. "Imagine if I became a regular."

"There's not enough fountain soda in London to make it worth either of our while," he said. He handed me a pint slammed to the brim with dark cola and ice. I took a tentative sip, then put my finger to my throat.

"Hmm—still alive," I said.

"Strychnine doesn't get in until next Monday," he said. "So: what's up?"

"Can we talk privately?"

Bowering told the other bartender—young guy, with stovepipe black jeans and a beard struggling somewhere between scruff and aspirational—to take ten, then made a sweep of the bar with his arm. We were, save for the cigarette burns on the seats and the yellowing posters in chipped frames, now alone. He leaned forward, resting his log-like forearms on the bar and bringing himself to my eye line.

"OK, then," he said. I could smell the cheap gel in his brush-cut hair as his head loomed close to mine. "Let's talk."

"You still taking bets?"

"A man's gotta make a living," he said.

"I'm trying to track a guy down, he's in the same line of work. A buddy of mine owes him a lot of money. I need to arrange a payment plan."

"Well, first, I wouldn't say it like that. You're not meeting with some bank teller, trying to get a better mortgage rate here."

"You know what I mean."

"I do, I do. I've had the pleasure of talking with you before. But maybe try not to sound like a professor all the time. Might work out for ya."

"Thanks for the advice. But I come by it a bit too honestly. My mom gave me lots of books as a kid."

"Let me guess: they were your friends when things were tough."

"Things were tough a lot. Still are. So, you going to help me or not?"

Bowering chuckled, not unkindly. "Sure. What the hell. Who's the guy?

"Alphonse Quigley."

Bowering topped up my Coke.

"Your mate's into that mad Irishman? He must be desperate."

"If you mean he was drowning in debt, made a lot of bad choices and had nowhere else to go, then yeah, desperate pretty much covers it."

"I know Alphonse. I got a number for one of his leg men, and my guys have helped him once or twice. But you'd probably be better off seeing him in person."

"Where is he?"

"Well, it's not like he's got office space in the Mile," Bowering said. "But I know a few places he hangs out."

I got out my notebook.

"Your best bet's this curry house he hits most Fridays, place called the Empress," Bowering said. "Last I heard he and his crew book out the room in the back."

"Can you reach out, let 'em know I'm coming?"

He shook his head. "I know the guy. But not like that. For first steps, you're on your own."

"Roger that," I said. I pulled out my phone and looked up the Empress' address, adding it to my notes.

"Get there early, before the fourth or fifth round of Cobras," Bowering added.

"Anything else I should know?"

"Yeah," he said. "Don't be a smart-arse. This guy's not messing around. He won't be as impressed with your business card or dry wit."

"You were impressed?"

"I was patient, Grayle," Bowering said. "Very patient. Plus, you gave me money. That smooths over a lot of cracks."

"That I did. Speaking of…?" I mimed reaching for my back pocket.

Bowering shook his head.

"No, no money."

"Well, that's refreshing. I'm pleased with your sense of community service."

Bowering shrugged. "What can I say? You gotta give back. Plus, if I'm being honest, I need a favour, too."

"Oh yeah? What's on your mind?"

Bowering curled one hand's thick fingers around the back of his neck and began kneading.

"I need you to run a check on someone in my employ," he said.

"Sure," I said. "How deep you looking for? Basics, like credit rating and last couple of jobs, or we talking the all-out, unabridged Russian novel?"

"How long for the full *War and Peace*?"

"Could be weeks. But months, more likely."

"What can you get in a week?"

"Well, I'm going to have to farm it out. I'm up to my hips in this and another case. But I know someone. She's new, but good. She can find out a lot, but I can't guarantee you the results on a strict timeline. Some people are open books, 'cause they don't really have anything to find. Others are good at picking up all the breadcrumbs."

"You trust this person?"

"Oh yeah," I said. "Absolutely."

Bowering considered this. What he was really wondering was if he could trust me.

"OK," he said. "One week, and we're square."

We shook again.

"Who's your area of concern?" I asked.

He flicked his head towards the entrance, where his colleague had left after being dismissed.

"That guy," he said. "Name's Tom Raynott. He came on a few weeks back."

"What, that kid? What's the problem?"

"Nothing. He seems OK. Good bartender. But I need to pick up a few guys for some other stuff and I don't know enough about him to, you know, bring him in."

He pulled an accordion box from under the bar, rifled through it, and handed me Raynott's resume, plus a paystub with his national insurance number. I gave it all a quick once-over.

"You should pay people more," I said.

"He does great with tips. Look, can you help or not?"

I laughed. "Relax, man. I'm messing with ya. Yes, I said can help."

Bowering worked his neck a bit more. He obviously wasn't used to dealing with outside contractors. Or asking anyone for help at all, I would imagine.

"I can get you something," I said, attempting to appease. "But this stuff you're asking for help with—if the kid is clean, is this going to get him in trouble?"

Bowering considered his response for a moment before giving it.

"He can always say no."

"Fair enough," I said, stuffing the papers into my jacket. "Anything else?"

"Yeah," he said, pulling back from the bar and assuming his

48

full height. And width. "Mine is a trust-based enterprise. That's why I need to know the kid's all right. It's also why I don't feel great letting you poke around in my business."

"It's in my interest to do this and do it well," I said. "You're a good source to have."

"Let's keep it that way. Like I said, I know Alphonse. And I know the guys he uses to express his…disappointment. I know they're always looking for extra work."

"You're threatening me?" I asked, mock horrified. "I would think that was beneath you."

"It's important to have clear boundaries," he said, grabbing a towel and getting to work on some wet highball glasses. "And I like to keep all my relationships uncomplicated. Especially business ones."

"Then trust me to do my job," I said, standing.

"Christ, I barely trust you at all," he said. "So go win me over, will ya?"

10

My office, later that night. Over the last few months I had spent more and more time here, both out of necessity—as I was now responsible for all my paperwork and appointments, it was eating into actual work time—and boredom. Work was a great distraction, and there was plenty about. Any work fiend will tell you there's always something more to be done—a shrink would have a field day with me transferring my previous bad habits into, say, revamping my filing system or scrubbing old files from my laptop.

Ayesha arrived with her cappuccino and an easy smile. She kept even worse hours than me, so she didn't mind when I had called her to come over. I gave her the rundown on the Bowering job, and she quickly agreed—one week, standard freelance rate.

"You must like this guy to do a freebie for him," she said.

"It's not free. It's a bit of quid pro quo. Besides, he and I, we go back a bit."

"Are you getting sentimental?"

"No, quite the opposite—painfully practical. Speaking of, you hearing anything more about the Duclos thing?"

She shook her head. "All my sources are quiet on it. If he's alive, he's done a damn good job going undercover."

"And we still have zero idea of his motive or state of mind."

"Pretty much, yeah. What'd the wife say?"

I stirred my coffee.

"That he quietly and expertly stole 4 million quid over the last few years from his employers and clients, information she is withholding from the police. Hence hiring me to find him first."

I sipped, then watched. Her face was quizzical for a split second, then her eyes went wide as a pair of hubcaps.

"Daaaaaamn," she said, and she threw her head back with a throaty laugh.

I couldn't help laughing too.

"I know, right?" I said. "Pretty bad-ass. I think I like her, too, actually. God knows she's got a set of brass ones on herself."

"So, what did she give you?"

I pointed to the folder on my desk.

"Pretty thick," she observed.

I shook my head. "Most of it is financials. Not a lot on his personal life or his friends. Or more importantly, enemies."

"Guy steals a few million, he's going to have some enemies."

"I dunno. Everything so far speaks to how smart he is—I am not really feeling him as sloppy or foolish. Not yet, anyhow. I asked the wife how she found out about the money. She said—get this—'He told me.' That was it. She says she had no idea. When she asked why he only said that it was for the future."

"Someone knows. You'd better find that person before the cops do. Or maybe you'd prefer to keep wrestling with that." She nodded towards the folder.

I sighed.

"I don't suppose you're a forensic accountant as well?" I asked.

"Don't be greedy," she said. "I bring enough to the table for my clients."

"You'll hurt my feelings, talking about other suitors."

"It's for the best. I think it's important to be upfront about these things." She leaned back, crossing her legs at slender ankles. "But I do know a guy, actually. Clem Mattingly. Heard of him?"

I shook my head. I was plugged in, but Ayesha was on another level. Her freelance security and bodyguard work was primarily for the type of people who had hospital wings and school buildings named after them—while they were still alive.

"Used to work for AGI, left early 2008," she filled me in.

"Before the crash?"

"Yup. He says he saw it coming, but I think he was just lucky. He has his own shop now for some exclusive clients. He's good, and if I asked, he'd take a look. It won't be cheap, though."

"I appreciate your honesty, even when I know what's coming," I said, I leaned back, drumming my fingers on the file. "There was something," I said. "There's a pile of family pics all over the place, her and the hubby and their kid. There was one pic of Mr. Duclos on a boat with some guy."

"Boat?"

"Yacht, I think. They had these big entitled smiles and were smoking cigars, both of which would be very yacht-like behavior."

"Could be a start. Otherwise it's the folder and homework all weekend for Mr. Grayle."

"Funny you should say that. I was at a school today, if you recall. Chatting with the Duclos kid."

"Oh yeah? What's he like? Completely insufferable or just quietly messed up?"

"Quietly messed up, at least according to all the evidence I've seen. Nice kid though. Seems pretty twisted up all over this."

"Well, yeah. Imagine your dad just ups and vanishes. Bit of an abandonment rug pull, I'm guessing."

"Sure, yeah," I said. "But… I don't know. He's definitely a little weird. Intense, too. And a loner. Or maybe just lonely."

"How's that?

"I walked him through the school at recess to go somewhere quiet to chat. I wanted to see him in his environment. Not one kid said hello to him."

"Ouch. How old is he?"

"Old enough to know how much that sucks."

"What were you like in school?" she asked.

"I was a pretty good student. But I was bored a lot. If I wasn't interested in something, I rarely tried my best."

"Did that help prepare you for adult life?" she asked, nodding towards the financials and adding a just wicked-enough smile to accentuate her point.

"Until I went into this racket and had the pleasure of such acquaintances as yourself," I sweetly demurred. She laughed again, giving me the chance to switch gears back to the topic at hand.

"The kid, though. He definitely left me with the impression all was not great at home. The marriage might be chilly, or the dad might be nasty. But he wouldn't really give me much more. I didn't want to push too hard, either."

"You were a teacher, right? You good with kids?"

I considered this for a moment. In my office desk, in the top drawer just to my right, there was a framed picture, facing up, of Amy and me from last Boxing Day. She had loved the chess set I gave her—and she hated I had left early.

I said it was work. It had been. Paperwork and notes. But it could've waited.

"Some," I said. "And only sometimes."

11

According to a quick text exchange with Annie Duclos, the guy in the yacht photo was Daniel Worster, another big shot at Bergman Hapsburg. He and Duclos had worked together for years in the Mile and were, at least according to Mrs. Duclos, both comrades-in-arms in the morally barren terrain of international high finance, as well as occasional pub buddies on Fridays. In other words: friends. And "friend" was not a word I was hearing a lot about in reference to Yannick Duclos.

I followed Worster from his office to that pub, watching his easy manner with the bartender and his waves to fellow 5 o'clock regulars. It was still pretty quiet in there but knowing the Mile's inhabitants and their predilection towards excess, I wasn't willing to risk sitting back much longer. I slid onto the stool next to him, unbuttoning my jacket and waving to get the barman's attention.

"You might have to try a bit harder," Worster said, sipping his first pint. "Phillip can be a bit slow sometimes. But he makes up for it in personality."

"That's OK," I said. "He's not going to be too excited whipping me up a club soda anyways."

"So, not a big night, then?"

"Those are well behind me," I said, twisting to face him. "I'm Thad."

We shook hands. As he began to introduce himself, I responded by handing him my card. He barely glanced at it before gracing me with a sad little head shake.

"I know who you are," I said, "and you're a man I want to talk to."

"Goodness," he said, getting back to his pint but still giving me the once-over. "Not sure how I feel about being... *stalked.*"

"In my line of work, we just call it research. Annie Duclos has hired me to help find her husband."

To his credit, he didn't even flinch.

"How's that going?" he asked.

"Just taking the deep dive into his life. Which is why you and I are making small talk before I can actually get rolling here."

"Ask away," he said.

"Do you know any reason why Yannick would want to disappear?"

Worster shrugged. "None. I mean, he was under a lot of stress and work was hectic, but he never the type to grumble."

"So when you guys got together, you'd talk about…"

I waited for him to jump in. Instead, he took another swig.

"Hey," I said. "Feel free to jump in here. This isn't playtime. Your guy is missing and I'm trying to find him."

"I already spoke to the police," he said.

"And I've been hired to assist in that investigation," I said, my voice rising a few decibels. "You can call Mrs. Duclos to confirm all this."

"Oh, I will," he said. "As well as to ask why on earth she's hired some penny-ante gumshoe to faff about in all this when the police are likely far more capable."

I smiled at Worster, waiting him out. Phillip, the barman, finally made his way over to me.

"Club soda, lime," I said. "Cheers."

Neither of us said anything until my drink arrived a few moments later.

"Perhaps that was somewhat unkind," Worster finally allowed. "But honestly, I'm shocked to be talking to you. This is preposterous."

"Exactly how so?"

"The police are no doubt sparing no resource in their investigation. This is at best, a waste of time. At worst, you're actively meddling in their pursuit."

"I'm not going to get into their way. Mrs. Duclos just wanted some extra help, including your presumed cooperation in this conversation as a family friend. So, again: What'd you guys talk about when you'd hang out?"

"Work. Our kids. Money. Women."

"The usual, then."

"Once you get to a certain age, the range of topics narrows considerably."

"Did he have any enemies?"

Worster rolled his eyes by way of shaking his head.

"OK, on your topic of women, then. Did Duclos mess around?"

No eye roll this time, but a short snort.

"Yannick? No. Never. I don't think he even thought about it. His was a...quiet existence, for the most part."

"He sounds like a real fun guy to spend your Fridays with, then."

Worster shifted on his stool, catching Phillip's eye for round two.

"Look, we were work friends. We didn't grow up together and we weren't veterans of some great war together. We moved money around to make more of it. He was good at it. And he was, in my observation, a good person, full stop. So maybe he wasn't a sparkling conversationalist. Good people are hard to come by."

Phillip arrived with Worster's pint. He took a deep sip and gave me a glance.

"But, as I'm sure you will agree, there's more to life than small talk, detective."

"Was that your yacht? The one you two were on last year in that photo?"

"Hardly. I'm rich, but not ridiculously so. Not yet, anyhow. No, that was Klodjan's boat. We were out fishing, drinking, carousing."

"Who's that?"

"Klodjan Copta. A client. Very well off. *He's* the kind of person who owns a yacht, and lots of other big-boy toys."

"What's he do for a living?"

"He has many interests, but his primary corporation deals with property development and real estate."

"Was this a regular thing, you guys all getting together?"

Worster thought this over.

"Maybe once or twice a year. He was always willing to demonstrate his gratitude."

"Sounds like a helluva guy. I think I should meet him."

"You can reach his office through the magic of any number of internet search engines," Worster said, finishing his second.

"You know," I said, "Normally I'd offer to spot you a round for your trouble, but based on our conversation I worry you might find the offer insulting."

"Not nearly as insulting as something that has just occurred to me," he said.

"What's that?"

"It occurs to me you know more than you're letting on. Annie wouldn't have hired someone like you if there wasn't a reason for it."

"I told you the reason."

"Please," Worster said. "You don't have to tell me, but don't patronize me."

"What makes you so sure?" I said, tugging a fiver loose from my coat and tucking it under my glass.

"Annie and Yannick were the two most straight-laced and somewhat boring people I know," he said. "For her to go outside the norms of this investigation and engage with a private detective… Well, it tells me something else is going on."

"Maybe *you'd* like to be a detective."

"I don't know," Worster replied, raising his glass in farewell. "How's the pay?"

"Not great, but the perks are OK," I said, standing and turning away. "You don't have to talk to people any longer than absolutely necessary."

12

The next day. An afternoon of tailing Klodjan Copta had demonstrated a few of his passions—his Rolls, the racetrack, a lovely wine bar in the West End—but little about his work. If he had an office, this may very well have been his day off. Or maybe he was at the point in his life and career where the money just somehow happened. Either way, calling his offices seemed a bit of a dice roll, so I decided to take the more forward approach.

He was just wrapping up lunch, a Turkish spot on Holloway Road. Hardly high-end, but still decent. His driver held the door for him as I made my move to catch his attention.

"Mr. Copta?"

He was about halfway in, and his head snapped up at the sound of his name, his eyes appraising me quickly. The driver kept his arm on the door, effectively a barrier between his boss and me, the interloper.

"Yes?" he asked. "If this about work, I'd prefer if you would call and make an appointment."

"It is work—but mine, I'm afraid." Deciding against reaching over, I handed my card to the driver, who passed it on. Copta studied it for a moment, and his features relaxed.

"I have a feeling I know what this is about."

"I was pretty certain you were a smart person," I said, tilting my head to the restaurant. "I've had the stuffed peppers from this place. Pretty good."

"I have somewhere to be," he said. "If you don't mind getting a lift, we can talk in here if you want. Magnus, let him by."

I shrugged consent and approached the door, Magnus, the driver, finally letting me pass with the solemnity of Moses parting the waters.

The back was all leather and a lot of space. Copta lounged easily in his corner, clearly relaxed in his supple surroundings.

"Mr. Duclos," he said.

"In one," I answered. "I'm trying to find him, so I'm looking to get a picture of his life before he went missing."

"I wasn't really a big part of his life."

"Not really, but it's a start. Plus business is always fertile terrain, motive-wise."

Copta took that with a smile.

"I assure you, I had nothing to do with this."

I raised my hands. "Not my implication. But surely you know that following money in these matters is hardly a waste of time."

"For sure," Copta assented. "I'd be happy to show you our files and my history with Duclos and his firm."

"That'd be great."

"If you have a court order."

"Ah. Well, my approach is typically a bit more spontaneous."

"Not a fan of paperwork?"

"It's not my strong suit. Look, I can always go to the cops and ask what they have. Mrs. Duclos would be happy to vouch for me, and I assume you've spoken to them already."

"Then you hardly need my help in that regard," he said. "By all means, then, speak to the police."

Damnation. It had been worth a shot. Time for another approach.

"I will. But I'm trying to get a picture of Duclos as a man. Worster said you guys socialized on occasion."

"Yes, certainly. Nothing special. A few nights out, once or twice on my boat. They did good work, and I wasn't afraid to show my appreciation."

"Did that appreciation include booze and food, or anything a bit more salacious?"

Duclos shook his head, amused.

"I understand that your job description means you have to always assume the worst, but these were not men interested in much more than nice steaks and a decent Scotch. But there may be someone else you can talk to." He scribbled a name on the back of one of his cards, handing it over.

"I wrote that man a cheque last year. He went to school with Yannick, way back when. It was a fundraiser. Something for his daughter's…volleyball tournament, or some such. Yannick asked, and I was happy to oblige."

"Thanks," I said, palming the card.

He took a very obvious glance at his watch and sighed. Getting bored.

"Rolex GMT, right?" I asked. "The Pepsi? Nice piece."

He didn't even attempt to disguise his surprise. "You're a horology fan?"

"Nah, not really. My dad liked watches, I picked up a few bits and pieces along the way." I shot my cuff, rolling my wrist to show him mine: A battered Seiko diver that had served honourably for far too long. "My job means my taste has to tilt a bit more to the functional."

"Nothing wrong with that, Mr. Grayle," Copta said, pulling his French cuff back over the jubilee bracelet and two-tone bezel.

"What about Duclos? Did he like the fancy stuff?"

Again, Copta shook his head.

"Honestly, I have no idea what he did with his money," Copta said. "His suits were getting a bit frayed, he drove a ten-year old Honda, and I think my haircut cost more than his shoes. I'm not judging—there's no shame in frugality—but surely a man with a few pounds in the bank should treat himself every now and then."

Just a few pounds.

"Maybe he was worried about the future," I mused.

"Perhaps, but one should be allowed to enjoy the present," Copta said, making a short wave of his arm through the Rolls' air.

"I'm sure it's good for some," I said.

Copta laughed, a short, sharp chuckle. "Come now," he said. "You're doing more than all right, are you not?"

"Excuse me? I'm not sure I understand."

The car had begun to slow. We were, apparently, arriving.

"Yours is not a common name," Copta said. "One does not forget hearing it. And today was not the first time I had."

"Who, me?" I said. "I'm a nobody. I'm the grey man."

The driver popped the door on my side first, and stood, somehow both stiffly and impatiently.

"There are a lot of colours in this world," Copta said as I slid out. "And a lot of masks for a man to wear. In my experience, they all fit. Enjoy the rest of your day, Mr. Grayle."

13

The Empress was tucked away deep in the East End, a neighbourhood now more famous for its bohemian art scene and cuisine than the slums and disease that had marked it as recently as the late 1800s. Gentrification takes no prisoners, least of all memories, good or bad.

True to Bowering's heads-up, Quigley and some of his crew were assembled in a private room in the back. I held back a bit, waiting for one of the waiters to appear with a tray of poppadoms and another with a full round of pale ales. I slipped in behind him, content to wait while the fuel was distributed. I was noticed soon enough.

"Help you?" one of Quigley's boys asked, pasty and stuck with an unruly mop of red hair. He was heaping a load of rice and curry onto still-warm naan bread.

"I'm hoping so," I said, making eye contact with the ruddy-faced man at the head of the table.

My interrogator turned to his boss. Quigley shrugged.

"Go ahead," Quigley said. "But let's keep it quick, all right?"

Quigley was pale, oil-drum chested with sandy-brown hair reduced to stubble, ground to his scalp through a pitiless buzz cut. His arms were freckled, ropy pillars, the numerous tattoos faded through time and sun. He wiped his mouth and took a heavy swig of beer.

"Friend of mine owes you money," I said. "Taylor Brock. I'm here to let you know it will get taken care of."

"Well, that is just wonderful news. Thanks for stopping by," he said. His cohorts chuckled.

"There are terms," I said. "We need some time. I'm here to ask for it."

Quigley gave a nod to one of the other apes he was eating

with. He stood and closed the door.

"What's your name?" Quigley asked me as he returned to his curry.

"Grayle."

He shoveled food into his mouth, barely stopping to chew.

"What do you do, Grayle?"

"This and that," I said. "I like to think I'm a man of a few talents."

"A real Renaissance man. I hear ya," he said.

The others were not eating. They were staring at me, gazes slackened ever-so-slightly by a few drinks—but not by much.

"Well, this is what I do," Quigley continued, still eating. The man to his left pushed another plate of korma towards him. "I lend people money. Those people pay me back or they get hurt. Then I still get paid, but it's usually more for my trouble and my crew's. Do you understand?"

"Yes."

"Your man Brock, he owes me how much?"

He obviously knew, but wanted to hear me say it, give what may feel like an abstract number life, as grim as it might be.

"Eight grand."

"And you're here why?"

"To assure you that you will get paid. We just need a bit more time."

"How much time?"

"Week," I said. "Maybe even less."

"He could've come here himself. Why'd he send you?"

"He didn't. I offered."

"Let me guess," he said, finally looking up from his food. He reapplied the napkin to his thick lips. "You're helping your friend out."

"Pretty much, yeah."

"Where you from, Grayle?"

"I live near Holloway, but I'm guessing you mean originally. U.S. of A. Pacific Northwest."

This gave him pause, then a smile.

"You like the rain or something?"

"It's my delicate complexion," I said. "Not made for the

sun."

"Well, that's a possible upside to all this for you," he said. "Because if I don't get my money in five days, you and Brock will be far, far away from sunlight."

"Like I said, we might need a week."

Quigley retuned to his plate. Two of his guys stood and took me by the arms.

"Hey," I said. "I'm being reasonable here. C'mon."

One of them snapped my arm tight against my back, pushing the hand close to the shoulder blade. The other rummaged in my pockets, throwing my wallet to Quigley.

"Thaddeus Grayle," he said, pulling my driver's license. "202A Seven Sisters Road, London. Hunh."

"What's the problem?"

"I dunno," he said. "That's a nice suit. And not a great neighbourhood."

"It's close to the Tube," I said, trying not to sound defensive. "Plus, there's some nice restaurants."

I was released. I resisted the urge to rub my sore wrist. He rummaged further into the wallet's folds.

"Private investigator," he read from my license. "My oh my."

"It's a living," I said.

"Bad choice of words," he said. "Considering the circumstances."

He nodded to an empty seat across from him at the table. I took it.

"Brock's already late," he said. "The interest has climbed substantially. Did he tell you that?"

I sighed, inwardly. "Not in so many words, no."

"Some detective."

"I've been getting better."

"Be terrible if your progress stalled, then," he said. He pushed a plate towards me. I forked some paneer to my mouth. He gave me a chance to chew before continuing.

"All right, Miss Marple, this is how we're going to proceed: In five days, you will bring sixteen thousand pounds here. You will hand it to one of my boys and then you and Brock will piss off. Mightily so. I don't want to ever see you or his miserable gob ever again."

"Wait. I don't suppose I could challenge your math."

He waved this away.

"This isn't a negotiation. Frankly, I'm insulted Brock couldn't come here himself."

"As he and I are partners with this, I thought it best to introduce myself."

"Because you're vouching for him. And this money."

I nodded.

"OK, then. But know this: If in five days you've not come through that door with sixteen thousand pounds, there will be, as my teachers used to say, consequences for that choice."

I nodded again.

"In the next few days we are going to figure you out, poke around in your life a bit. We know where you live, we know what you do, so we're going to go ahead and start making a list of things that are were precious to you. These may or may not include your legs, but what the hell. I might just start with those and figure the rest as I go. Which will include any money in this little business you got going for yourself."

"How's that?"

Quigley grinned. "I'm guessing a fella like yourself knows a lot of bad people with bad secrets. They can be bled, too. People come up with all sorts of money when it comes to hiding the truth."

I sighed.

"Can't we keep this just between us?" I asked. "I'd still like to make a living when this is all settled."

"No. Because this debt is on you now, too. And because this is how I make *my* living."

"Well, I guess we're all clear on the stakes, then."

"I hope so," he said. "Because you just co-signed a loan for a complete degenerate. I actually feel bad for you."

I ate some more paneer, trying to prove I could eat around the growing tumble of dread knotting my guts.

"Why's that? It's my neck to risk, Quigley."

"No, I meant you must be pretty hard up if this guy is what

passes for a friend in your life." He gave his head a small shake. "Anyhow. Food good?"

"Yeah. It's not bad."

"Great. Good to hear. Now get out. Back to your mate, then."

I took a turn wiping my own mouth, going a little slower than usual. Finally, I stood, and turned for the door. I didn't even see the guy standing in front of me, same guy who first spoke to me, as he drove his fist deep into my solar plexus. I dropped straight to my knees, sucking wind.

"Just to clarify," Quigley said. "It's important the stakes, as you put it, were absolutely clear. I am not a bank. I am not American Express. I do not have negotiable payment options."

I stood, a bit shaky, but not bad.

"That, and it was pretty rude of you to just drop in," he said. "So, we all clear?"

"Yup." It came out like a hiss, but it still made its way clear of my lips.

"You can't talk your way out of everything, Grayle," he said, getting back once more to his meal. My wallet was stuffed back into my pocket as I was roughly shoved through the door. "Now me—well, I like a bit of silence, from time to time."

14

Copta had connected me with Elmore Cranston, who was more than a little surprised by my approach as he queued for his morning coffee before heading to work. He was in a natty, if slightly out-of-style suit, careful not to get any foam on it as he blew a little steam from the top of his cappuccino.

"You work in finance, too?" I asked.

"Sort of," he said, as we exchanged cards. He was an insurance agent.

"So, how far back did you and Duclos go?" I asked we stepped out onto Admirals Way, heading towards his office in East London.

He smiled, a sad little thing. "Long time. We were school chums."

"You guys close?"

He shook his head. "No, life has a way of getting in the way. You know how it is. Get married, have a kid, lots of your own life stuff starts falling by the wayside."

"What I've been hearing, Duclos didn't have a lot of friends."

Cranston sighed. "He was a quiet guy."

"You know any reason he'd just up and disappear?"

"Not now, no. His life looked pretty good the last time we talked."

Cranston had a long stride. I picked up my pace a bit.

"When was that?" I asked.

"Year ago? We met for lunch. Outside of a birthday text, I don't think I'd spoken to him since."

"What'd you guys talk about?"

"Um… work, I guess. Football. Duclos is a Chelsea supporter."

"So nothing out of the ordinary? Nothing stands out?"

Cranston regarded me with some mix of curiosity and disdain.

"Well, he didn't exactly floor me with his stories. Sorry to disappoint."

"Sorry," I said. "But it seems like I'm working the case of the quietest missing person I'd ever have imagined."

"If you haven't found him yet, he obviously doesn't want to be found," Cranston said.

"Yeah, I've been getting a lot of that. What was he like as a kid?"

"Sporty. Shy. Decent student. Never Mr. Popularity, but he was respected, I think. He did very well with rugby."

"Where'd you guys go to school? Anywhere good?"

"Good enough," he said. "Yannick certainly did all right for himself."

"Yeah, about that," I said. "You ever worry that was maybe why you guys drifted apart?"

He stopped.

"How's that?" he asked.

I shrugged.

"You know," I said. "He goes off and becomes some big-time financier, big house, lots of money, gets to spend time on yachts. And you sell home insurance."

Cranston's jawline went hard and sharp.

"I do all right," he said.

"Sure, but, you know, not West Brompton all right."

"Yannick wasn't like that," he said. "And this is beyond insulting, both to him and me."

"Look," I said, my own jaw setting a bit. "Nothing is shaking loose on this guy, and I can't help but think as his only childhood friend that you might know something a bit more. So pardon me for hurting your feelings."

"Yannick had a lot of class. More than you're showing now. He helped my daughter raise money to travel for her volleyball team. They were selling chocolate bars and he bought a crate. He even hit up his clients for cash."

"Yeah, I met one of them. He could have drove that entire team to those games, the back of his Rolls was that big."

Neither of us had started walking again. Cranston raised his cup to his face, peering at me over the lid. I took the opportunity to listlessly glance around, waiting for him to work through any possible lingering career disappointment.

"Maybe you're shaking the wrong trees," he finally said. "Maybe someone else needs some tough questions."

"How so?"

"There weren't a lot of people Yannick was close to. Maybe there weren't any people he was close to."

"He was married, Elmore."

"Yes," he said, acidly. "He was."

That was all he said. He then walked away, happy to be rid of me, leaving me to politely sidestep the other denizens of the sidewalk, leaving me to feel poorly for more than my manners.

15

In my experience, outside of Calloway at least, cops were the absolute worst in calling people back. I had left a message and e-mail for DI Dunsmore shortly after meeting up with Ian, but she had yet to follow up. I found her pic on LinkedIn and spent the morning pacing outside the Met HQ in Whitehall, keeping one appreciative shop owner in more than a few quid for a coffee and two refills. Finally, shortly before 11, Dunsmore appeared, exiting the building and chatting with a colleague. I made my move as she said good bye and stepped to her car.

"So you're Grayle," she said after I introduced myself.

"Afraid so. Got a minute?"

"Barely." She glanced at my coffee. "But then again, I wouldn't say no to one of those."

"My pleasure," I said, and we stepped across to the caf. I tipped big, earning an appreciative smile from the owner. She carefully poured half a packet of sugar into her coffee, stirring it in slowly. I waited until she was done. We sat.

"You know the Duclos wife has hired me to help with the investigation," I said. "So I'm just looking to introduce myself, swap info, see if we can't help each other out a bit."

"We typically advise against families seeking private assistance in these matters."

"That why you dodged my voicemail?"

She shook her head.

"Nothing discourteous. Just not a lot going on with this case as of yet, and lots going on with others."

Dunsmore was very tall—I'd say pushing 6 feet—and had shoulders broad enough that her pantsuit jacket was struggling a bit at the seams. She clearly had some serious athletic experience in her past.

"Am I right in assuming you're lacking a sense of urgency here, DI?" I asked.

Again, another shake of the head.

"It's all about resource allocation," she said. "You know what happens when someone reports a missing person to us?"

"My previous missing person experience was a bit off the proverbial track, so you'll have to fill me in a bit."

"We ask if the person is in immediate danger. Mrs. Duclos said yes. We contacted her immediately, interviewed her, but frankly, I can't see any risk. Therefore, the case loses precedence to other life-and-death investigations."

"She seems pretty busted up about it."

"Of course," Dunsmore said, not without sympathy. "It's her husband. But look at it from our perspective, Mr. Grayle. A rich man goes missing, cleans out his bank accounts, and leaves not a single message of his whereabouts. In our experience, that means he doesn't want to be found."

"Yeah, I get that, but… why?"

She smiled a bit, and I wondered if Dunsmore wasn't enjoying feeling like my learned elder.

"Lots of reasons. Running from debt. Running from responsibilities. Running from a life he may not want. He wouldn't be the first wealthy, middle-aged guy to pull this move."

"So, as for the current status of this investigation, you'd describe it as—"

"What do you have?" she interrupted. "You got anything new or interesting on this?"

I put on a practiced air of resignation, which was, to be fair, only half-faked.

"Not a thing. Guy was a loner. Not likely he had any real enemies. But like you said—maybe he just wanted to disappear. I read something in *The Atlantic* about this—male mental health issues at an all-time high, massive upswing in depression, lots of guys doing themselves in."

"Well, there's no evidence that he killed himself," she countered. "He did clean out his accounts, remember. So he obviously has some sort of plan, or at the very least, the goal of staying alive for at least the foreseeable future."

"So… we'll find him when we find him?" I asked.

"I'm confident he'll turn up, eventually. We are investigating, but for now—not our top priority."

"Well, thanks for this," I said. "I know I kept you, so I appreciate it."

"No worries, happy to help," she said. "But please do keep us posted on anything you might uncover in your own pursuits." She handed me her card.

I made a show of studying it.

"How'd you become a copper, DI Dunsmore?" I asked.

"Oh, I don't know," she said. "All the usual reasons, I suppose. Wanted to help people. Wanted to make a difference. Liked *Prime Suspect.*"

"I hear ya. How do any of us become the things we end up being?"

"One thing just follows another. It's a bit scary, really."

"I think that every kid should get that as a warning, soon as they turn 13, crocheted on a pillow or maybe printed on a t-shirt," I said.

"To mark the end of childhood. I get it."

I glanced at her left hand. Dunsmore was married.

"You got kids?" I asked.

"Two. Boy and girl, 10 and 8. You?"

"Girl. 14. She lives in Switzerland with her mom. Geneva."

"That's tough."

I shrugged. "This is where a lesser man might say 'it is what it is.'"

"You're taking the high road. Commendable."

"21st century families aren't all Rockwell paintings," I said. "Besides, I hear you're a bit of an up-and-comer. Must be tough on your family life, too."

"Balance is key," she said, measuring her words. "Balance is everything."

She fell silent. I had possibly overstepped. I backtracked.

"Well, again, thanks," I said, standing and extending my hand. She shook it. Firm grip, and the hands were nowhere near soft.

"You're my first PI," she said. "We don't usually overlap with you lot that often."

"Well, I used to chase cheating spouses. Made a pretty good living from it."

"I had heard that was pretty lucrative. Why the change?"

"I thought I had enough of seeing people at their worst."

"So what's different now?" she asked. We stepped back into the street and I walked her to her car, her keys jingling in stride.

"Not much, really," I said. "But that's OK. The universe doesn't care about our attempts at self-improvement. And neither do our bills."

16

Later that night. Ayesha had arrived and I buzzed her in—apparently there was progress in her tail job on Bowering's bartender that needed reporting, as well as an update on the Yannick Duclos' financials. I was online, researching as much as I could about Mrs. Duclos—I felt there might be more there for me to dig into, following Cranston's comment. I was also, admittedly, restless.

Despite entering what I considered a relatively tidy apartment, Ayesha rolled her eyes as she slid into my well-worn easy chair.

"You live like a student," she said, surveying the bland interior and piles of old CDs and magazines on the floor.

"Hey, you've been here before," I said. "Why the sudden scorn?"

"We know each other a bit now. I don't have to play super-nice all the time."

"Speaking of—" I said, nodding towards her takeaway bag. She had picked up a chicken burger and Coke from the shop across the street.

"What?" she said. "You're big boy. Get your own treats."

"Well, it'd be nice to welcome visitors bearing gifts on occasion."

"I'm not you guest, and I am not your secretary," she said. "I am, however, on the clock."

I carried my laptop form my desk to my couch, clearing a neat row of empty diet soda cans and a bowl of crisps from the coffee table before laying it down.

"My attention is yours, wholly undivided," I said. "Let 'er rip."

"So, Bowering's guy checks out. Pretty straight kid. Has a girlfriend, but no outrageous social issues I can see. Goes to work, goes home, sees his mates a night or two at another pub."

"OK, then," I said. "He's hardly positioned to be brought into a life of crime and underworld intrigue."

"Agreed. From my observation, he seems resistant to temptation."

"How's that?"

"Well, he lives with another guy," she said. She opened her notes on her phone. "Kid named Fenske. This young man is a whole other matter."

She then took a hearty bite out of her burger. Say what you want about combat veterans' occasional lapses in social graces —they could tell a story. Really knew how to let the suspense build.

"Go on," I finally prodded.

She took a slug of her soda, just to irk me for a sec before jumping back in.

"Fenske is not nearly as well-behaved a young man. He has a lot of women coming in and out of the place, plus he deals. He uses a bit too, but nothing too crazy."

"What's he dealing?"

"Coke and H," she said. "His personal use is limited to coke. Maybe a little molly."

"So, standard young degenerate stuff. What's the issue? You said Raynott's squeaky clean."

"Well, here's the thing," she said, balling up her wax paper and again sipping deeply from the soda. "Fenske's supplier is a guy I know from some other jobs. This guy, Marshall Zanetti, is not an aspiring criminal. He is the real deal. And he moves a lot of heroin in this town. He and his crew have gone toe to toe with the Somalis and have carved out a pretty big swath of the recreational users in the posher SW postcodes."

"Posh like West Brompton," I murmured.

She nodded, smiling wide.

"So Duclos was using?"

"Oh, that I don't know. But I do know who Zanetti gets a lot of his product from."

"Do tell."

"The name Klodjan Copta mean anything to you?"

Copta—billionaire yacht owner, Rolex wearer and Turkish cuisine enthusiast.

"Yeah," I said. "It does. That was the guy Duclos was friends with. The photo I told you about."

"I know," she said, clearly pleased with herself. "I pulled a chunk of his financials, too." She pulled a folder from her bag and handed it to me.

"How'd you get this?" I asked.

"Friend of a friend. That's all I can say."

"Friend of a friend, as in, this is legally in your possession…?"

She leaned back in the chair, shaking her empty cup to hear the ice rattle. "Oh Thad," she said. "You're adorable."

I closed the folder and affected what I hoped was a non-adorable hardness to my face.

"Why don't you just give me the quick-and-dirty?" I asked.

"Well, he has a lot of irons in the means of production fire," she said, unfazed. "Shipping, mainly, but also some tech stuff. Real estate, too. From the looks of it, a lot of it is all legitimate. But he has been moving H for a long time and burying it in at least four shell companies. He might be a proud member of the ruling class now, but heroin is what got him started."

I had a sudden flashback to Copta's driver, Magnus, realizing that the man with the quiet demeanor and hawk-like gaze was also his protection.

"Might be something, might be nothing," I said quietly, more to myself than to her.

"You kidding? Your financial whiz Duclos goes missing, and he's friends with this guy. This guy, who he and his firm may been helping to keep a lot of money away from any authorities' prying eyes."

"So, what? Duclos was a user, became a problem, and they had to get rid of him?"

"Sure, that's one option."

The other landed, hard, in my still-tender gut.

"Or he screwed up," I said. "So they got rid of him."

She leaned forward, placing hands on top her knees.

"Thad," she said. "I don't know what you're getting paid here, but I hope it's a lot."

"It could be OK," I said. "In terms of the pay out."

"I just say it because right now your big lead is that the missing Duclos was maybe clipped following his possible deep involvement in a heroin money laundering ring."

"Yeah, I got it," I said. "You enjoying the dramatics?"

"Hey, I thought you'd be happy. This is some good legwork here."

"It is, for sure. Well done. But I'll make the decisions regarding the direction of these investigations."

She gave a nod of assent. Ayesha, to her credit, was never quick to take offense or stand on ceremony.

"You still thinking the wife angle?" she asked.

"Just something about how Cranston looked," I said. "Like there was a lot more to it all on the homefront."

"Husbands kill wives," Ayesha said. "Wives don't typically kill husbands. Plus, there's the money. He cleaned out their accounts."

I shrugged. "Maybe if someone did him in, they forced him to transfer all that cash."

"I suppose a PIN is small beer weighed against getting killed."

"Which we don't know even happened."

"Sure," she said, stretching. "I'm not entirely sold on the murder angle, either. But this is what we've got. So: who you gonna hit up first?"

"Mrs. Duclos," I said. "It'll be a short conversation, either way."

"You think she actually murdered him?"

"Not literally, no," I said. "But trust me. There's more than one way to kill a man."

17

Upon some consideration—undertaken in the time it took me to kick Ayesha out and drudge up something resembling a late dinner from the back of my fridge—I decided a different tactic would be needed to work the Mrs. Duclos angle. Hence me standing around outside this upscale yoga place a few blocks west of Sloane Square station early the next morning. The exiting clientele were uniformly female, slim and well-postured, despite what I had read was a furnace-like interior to help keep them limber during their poses. The rich even sweat better than we do.

I spotted Yvette Costley pretty easily. Even in this crowd, she stood out a bit. Despite being on the other side of 40 and an hour of hot yoga, she was summarily striking, making her way down Cale Street with her finishing school posture well intact.

She stopped to peer into a shop window, some vintage place with wooden trains going for 200 quid and mint-condition lifestyle magazines from the 1940s. I ambled next to her, pretending to be taking in some of the wares myself.

"Bit steep," she remarked.

"Oh, for sure," I replied. "But what's the price of a child's happiness?"

She nodded at an electric train set, coming in at just under a grand. "I think we may have just set it."

"Good thing mine has outgrown these things," I said. "Or was never interested."

"Lucky you," she murmured. She turned and faced me, drawing herself somehow a bit taller. "You're Mr. Grayle, I assume?"

"I am. Thanks for agreeing to see me."

"You were tough to turn down. You mentioned Annie and

her missing husband. I had seen something about in the paper. Dreadful stuff."

"Undoubtedly," I agreed. I had spent a few hours digging around Annie Duclos' social media presence when Ayesha finally got out last night, and Yvette was a good fit for what I needed: They had worked together in some online children's clothing boutique a few years ago, and shortly after had stopped popping up in each other's shared pics. In other words, an old, and possibly former, friend who had some knowledge but wasn't likely to run back to Annie with details of our chat.

I handed her a cold bottle of Evian.

"Thoughtful," she said, uncapping it.

"The best bribes usually are. But there's still door number 2." I tapped my suit's breast pocket.

"What do you want to know?"

"Like I said, I'm trying to find Yannick. But I'm thinking of looking a bit closer to home, first."

She unscrewed the cap and took a polite sip. In the early morning sun, there was still the gloss of her workout staining her forehead and throat.

"A marriage is a complicated thing, Mr. Grayle," she said.

"I know all too well. I guess I'm wondering if theirs was classically complicated or somewhat more unconventional."

"How so?" She took another sip, a deeper one.

"Do you think she might be interested in seeing him disappear?"

Yvette laughed.

"No, God no," she said. "Annie was a happy rich housewife, and those need husbands. Especially ones like Yannick."

"He was accommodating?"

"He was a mug. What I'm guessing you'd call a pushover."

"What was the problem?"

"Nothing, as long as he did what he was told. Look, Yannick was a good guy. Just a bit soft."

"I heard he had played a bit of sport when he was younger. Rugby. Doesn't sound too soft to me."

She rolled her eyes. "There's many a man who can easily stare down a real beating and not even flinch who would never imagine standing up to their wives."

"Was Annie particularly demanding?"

It was shortly after 8 a.m. Yvette took a glance around as the sidewalk was starting to crowd a bit.

"Annie usually gets what Annie wants," she said. "She ran that house. Yannick was happy to let her. He worked long hours and he wasn't always a lot of fun. He was moody a lot."

"Depression?" I asked.

"I'm no mental health professional, but I'd say so, yeah. I know she took off for a couple of weeks last year. Get some space."

"Did you ever hear of him talking about anything strange or unusual about work? Anything that stood out as maybe a bit shady?"

"Well, he was friends with that Copta guy. He didn't really talk about it, but Annie wouldn't shut up about the yacht and how rich the guy was."

This caught me.

"Annie knew Copta?"

Yvette nodded. "Oh yes. Apparently, they all socialized as families, a few times at least."

"Funny. Annie never mentioned that."

"Is it important?"

"Enh," I said, scratching my chin. I hadn't shaved that morning, and the stubble provided a satisfying bit of grit against the nail. "Probably not."

"So, I need to get going…" she said, directing her eyes to my pocket again.

"Sorry, not so fast. Did you ever know Yannick to, I don't know, get a bit carried away sometimes with, like, booze? Or other stuff?"

"No, never," she said. "I don't think I ever saw him have more than two glasses of wine whenever we were together."

I tugged the envelope loose, but not quite all the way out. Her eyes widened, ever so slightly.

"Why'd you and Annie fall out?" I asked.

"Who said we did?"

"My keen detective instinct," I replied. "As well as the fact that you sold your alleged friend out pretty cheaply."

She gave her shoulders an imperceptible shrug. If she felt badly, she was very good and not showing it.

"Sometimes when you're working with someone they can make you feel like you're working *for* them. Know what I mean?"

"Sure," I said, handing over the envelope. "That's why I enjoy being self-employed." She slipped it into her purse—two tickets to the opening night of *Love's Labour Lost,* courtesy Ayesha and a very happy client of hers from a bodyguard gig a few weeks back.

"Good seats," I said. "Enjoy."

"I will," she beamed. "Know what it's about?"

"I'm not really a Shakespeare guy."

"You might like it, considering your work. It's a comedy."

"I laugh plenty," I said.

"Yes, but in my experience, men rarely laugh at themselves," she said. "A major theme of it is how women threaten men's sense of self, their masculinity."

My phone buzzed—it was none other than Annie Duclos, seeking an update. I was thinking of how to best couch my response when I realized Yvette was still waiting on a response.

"Well, uh, we're famously sensitive about that," I said, a tad lamely.

She laughed. "Yes, no kidding. And rubbish at multitasking, as well. Nice to meet you, Mr. Grayle. Way to fight all the stereotypes."

18

That night. Brock and I had arranged for me to pick up the money at his place. I was looking forward to seeing him, putting his mind to rest a bit, so home was a good fit. Besides, there was no way I wanted to walk around with that much cash in what I assumed would be small denomination, crumpled bills, stuffed in a brown paper bag and likely damp from sweat. Maybe tears.

Ayesha bobbed back on forth on her heels as I hit the buzzer.

"How do you know this guy again?"

"Old friends," I said. No answer. I hit the buzzer again.

"AA?"

"I never went to AA much," I said. "I kinda just sweated it out."

"Literally and figuratively, I'm guessing."

"We all find our own way. He was big into it. Still is. Likes the structure." I fished my keys from my pocket. He had given me a set, long time ago. Back in our drinking days, I would crash here every once in a while.

"Letting yourself in?" she asked.

"Brock sometimes plays his music too loud. Or maybe he's taking a bath. Whatever. Let's go on up."

I switched the briefcase with my six grand around in my hand. It was heavy. Some of it was from a long-struggling line of credit from when I first opened shop. I had also kept some cash hidden in my place for emergencies, and it had been surreal stacking the bills neatly on my table. Reminded me of Jenga with my daughter, not least of all since Amy's tuition pay-out, this was pretty much the last liquid cash I had easy access to.

"Or maybe he's in trouble," she said.

"Don't be so dramatic," I said, calling him on my cell as we stepped towards the elevator. It rang a few times, then went to voicemail.

She shrugged. "You know him better than me," she said. "But if a buddy of mine were bringing me a lifesaving amount of money, I'd probably wait until he left to let Calgon take me away. Or whatever."

The door opened and we stepped inside. I switched hands again—my palms were a little damp.

Brock's place was on the 12th floor. The lift hummed to life, drawing us up.

"Anything more on Copta?" I asked.

"Everything I'm hearing is he's pretty hands off. Anything left to his dirty work is outsourced, naturally. And he's pretty much out of the game now, I reckon. Diversified."

"Why would drug trafficking be any different than anything else in this economy."

"You meeting him tomorrow? Want me to come?"

I glanced over.

"What?" she asked.

"Nothing. I had no idea you would worry, that's all."

"I'm not. You're a big boy. For my daily rate, though, I'll stand next to you and look menacing on a 40 million boat."

"I think it's closer to 50," I muttered. The lift lurched to a halt, and the doors opened.

No music blasting. I knocked on Brock's door. Still nothing. Ayesha nodded at my phone, still in my hand. I tried it. After a moment, we could hear something, low and thrumming, from inside.

"Let's go," she said. I quickly worked the key into place and popped the door. She stepped in front of me, hand instinctively going into her jacket.

The apartment was dark, empty—the kind of empty where people are nowhere to be seen and most everything was gone. Cleaned out. The furniture was still there, but anything personal that I had seen—photos of his kids, his framed law degree, a few souvenirs from last-minute cheap weekend getaways—were missing.

83

His phone trembled on his coffee table. I ended the call, stepping towards his bedroom.

"Hey," Ayesha said, putting her arm out to slow me. I shook my head and walked past her. There was no danger here. I was sure of it.

His room was the same—bed and rumpled duvet still there, but the nightstand was clear. I checked his closet—lot of clothes still left, but enough bare hangars to further let me know what was up.

I had hoped I was wrong, but is often the case in these matters, one was often disappointed by their correct instincts.

Ayesha and I reconnected in the living room. I walked over to the coffee table, picking up his phone. A few missed calls. Texts that would go unanswered, at least for a long time.

There was a yellow sheet of paper, A4, folded neatly in half next to it. I picked it up and opened it.

SORRY, MATE
-M

I let it fall back onto the table, where it fluttered before landing on its edge, falling closed.

"Thad?"

I said nothing. That couch over there, in the corner—I could still see the cigarette burn from one night we were here, drunk and laughing our asses off at a *Father Ted* marathon. He never bothered to swap it out, just put a cushion over it. You had to know it to see it, but there it was.

That kitchen, in front of the fridge. I had once opened the door, pulled out a beer, and without warning—even to myself—broke down crying in front of him. It was a week after Rox left. I felt both embarrassed and relieved when he grabbed me by the shoulders and said it was all going to be OK.

There was an empty frame on the bookcase. I knew the picture that was missing. It was him and his son. The kid would be about 14 now. I had stuck a 50-pound note into a birthday card for him, few years back. He had aced his report card. A June baby. Those could be tough when you were younger. School was out and you couldn't always get all the kids to come to your party. He was a good kid. I told him to get something stupid and fun.

"Thad? What's it say?"

"Nothing," I said, grabbing the phone and stuffing it into my jacket. Squeezing the case handle tight, I stepped towards the door, trying to fight the mounting wobble in my legs, the colour leaving my face. "Just that I'm fucked, is all."

19

"You ok?"

The next morning. Calloway had texted me late last night, keen to meet. Apparently he had some news regarding Dunsmore and her team. He was tucking heartily into a full English. We were in a caf on Green Lanes, one particularly well-regarded for its eggs-bacon-chips-beans combos. I had opted for a green tea and a booth seat that I could slouch in.

"Great," I said. "What's up?"

He pointed at my mug. "You going healthy or something?"

"All it takes is a few small changes for big results," I said. "What's up with the investigation?"

Calloway sprayed his plate with brown sauce. "How'd your chat with her go?

"Pretty good. I think she's all right, actually. Plus she made it clear there wasn't a lot going on in the case, so I've got some room."

He dipped his toast in yolk. I felt my stomach lurch.

"For a guy who deals with people's baser instincts and desires, your radar is a bit off," he said, taking a bite.

"I'm not following."

"Dunsmore and her team are all in on this. I told you, she's a mover and shaker."

Of course. I pressed my fingers into my eyelids. It wasn't like they could get much more bloodshot.

"So she was holding back? Or intentionally stalling me?"

"I don't know about the particulars," he said. "But it might be more likely they found something that has refocused their efforts."

"Like what?"

"Your man Duclos had some powerful friends. Guy by the name of Copta has been cooperating with the investigation."

"Wait, what? Klodjan Copta?"

He nodded.

"I don't understand."

"What's to understand? Apparently, Copta is a heavy hitter in Duclos's world. Big-time client. He wants the guy found. Came in and offered up his books that Duclos had worked on."

A chainsaw buzz was building in the back of my skull. I glared at my tea, resenting its lack of caffeine and satisfying bitterness.

"You sure you're OK?" he asked again.

"Yes. No. It doesn't matter. What else ya got?"

"You look pretty rough. You get any sleep last night?"

"Some. Calloway, c'mon. What are the cops saying about Duclos?"

He carefully doled out a heaping spoonful of sugar into his coffee.

"Might be something, might be nothing. But apparently he might've had some money socked away. Dunsmore has been in with the crew from fraud. But it's just a hunch."

The buzz grew.

"Oh God damn it," I whispered.

"This isn't helpful?" Calloway asked.

"In a manner of speaking, it is. In another, it is… disappointing."

Calloway considered this for a moment.

"You knew about the money," he said. I could see a touch of red blooming on his cheeks.

I effected my best sphinx face. I had it on good authority it was a solid one. Calloway, though, wasn't buying it.

"Jesus, Thad. You were going to get paid with the missing money?"

"I'm not confirming that, nor do I have to," I snapped. "And hey, maybe we should be a bit more upset that a major drug dealer is now your pal Dunsmore's best friend in all this."

"My superiors are framing it as assistance from an alleged and/or former dealer," Calloway countered. "I've been told to not be quite so boring with my outrage."

"Then let me get something here," I said. "Give me

something to work with."

Calloway lowered his fork.

"What's going on?" he asked.

"Nothing," I said. "Just, you know, I need some help here."

"You're holding out," he said. "I know it."

"Can you not treat me as a suspect, please?" I said. "Would it satisfy your keen investigative skills if I told you I was maybe in a bit of trouble and I really could use something like a lead so I can work this case?"

"What kind of trouble?"

I wasn't interested in Calloway's judgement or pity, and I was rapidly losing my patience. I got up to leave.

"Where you going?" Calloway asked.

"Work," I snarled. "My deadline has jumped ahead considerably."

Calloway forked some beans in his mouth, chewing thoughtfully.

"You know I started out in Camden, right? Beat cop?"

I slowed the pushing of my arms through my overcoat's sleeves.

"No," I said.

He nodded.

"Yeah," he said. "Back in the 90s heroin was everywhere there. Little blue bags. Tiny little things, really. Ten quid a score."

I sat back down. Calloway seemed disinterested in whether I was staying or going. Anyone looking on could be excused for thinking he might have been taking to himself.

"Blokes like Copta, they flooded the market," he said. "Price plunged. Heroin was the everyman drug now, right? Homeless guys. Beggars. Girls turning five quid tricks just to get halfway there."

I leaned in a bit closer. "Yeah?" was all I could think to say.

He nodded again, returning to his plate.

"Crazy, right?" he asked. "Just amazing. Anyhow, Copta seems a decent enough chap, or so I've been told. Lot of friends, they say. Heard he's having a party tonight, even."

"Ya don't say."

Calloway spread marmalade on some toast, plunging it into the yolk.

"Owns a yacht, too," he said. "Big ol' bash on it later on."

I waved to the waitress, signalling for the cheque. He shook his head.

"My turn," he said.

We sat in quiet for a moment, me waiting as Calloway fastidiously worked his way through the food.

"You know where that yacht is?" I finally asked.

He didn't even look up.

"St. Katherine's Docks, Tower Hamlets," he said. The waitress gave him the bill. "I imagine you'd just look for the biggest one there. You know, if you fancied dropping in to say hi, of course."

20

Unsurprisingly, Copta's taste in watches and cars extended to how he spent time on the water. His boat—the *Vivian*, according to the teak nameplate hanging from the stern—was huge. Admittedly, my yacht experience was minimal, but whatever we were standing on had three decks, a gym, a steam room and a massive sun deck. The inside was spacious and minimalist, and currently being roamed by people who were, I assumed, all a combination of rich, sleekly-clad and unnaturally thin. Ayesha snagged a flute of champagne from a passing tray. I asked for a sparkling water.

"Don't you own any cool clothes?" Ayesha asked. She was wearing a simple black cocktail number, cut a little longer in the skirt but still showing off enough leg to turn heads. Despite her somewhat rough-and-tumble professional experience, Ayesha could still roll in heels like a prom queen.

"What's wrong with this?" I said, patting a lapel on my somewhat rumpled herringbone three-piece.

"You look like a banker," she said.

"Great," I replied. "I'll fit right in, then."

"If we were at a party in 1985, sure," she finished, smiling sweetly behind her glass. "Seriously, how old is that thing?"

"Old enough. I'm not a big fan of change," I murmured, scanning the room. Copta was nowhere to be seen. Ayesha might be busy busting my chops but I could tell she was checking everything out as well. The kid was a pro. She gave a quick nod, and I followed her gaze. Copta was by the bar, holding court with a few of his fellow Masters of the Universe.

"Shall we?" I asked, extending my arm. She looped hers into the crook and we headed over to say hi.

"Mr. Grayle," our host said, genuinely surprised, but not offended. "How very good to see you again. And who might this be?"

"Ayesha Chantrill," she said, extending her hand. "I'm with Barclay's."

He took her fingers in his and gave a slight bow before kissing her knuckles.

"Absolutely charmed," Copta said. He turned to me. "It is my turn to compliment your taste, my good man."

"Oh, not at all," Ayesha said quickly. "I came after him so fast his head would've spun—if I could just get it out of all those case files."

Those gathered laughed politely, and I smiled, acquiescing in my role as the charming, if somewhat scattered, boyfriend.

"What can I say?" The waiter arrived, handing me my water, finally giving me something to do with my hands. "It's nice to be chased."

"Oh, I much prefer to be doing the chasing," Copta said. "There's something to be said for being on the prowl."

"Are we still talking about relationships or does that extend to business as well?" I said, smiling magnanimously.

Copta made a sweep of his arm towards the party, now starting to pick up its pace. "I think it's safe to say I'm not afraid to go for what I want, Mr. Grayle. I had my eye on a boat like this for some time, and finally pulled the trigger about a year ago. In my experience"—here his gaze lingered, just for a moment, on Ayesha — "patience and decisiveness go hand in hand."

"And on that topic," I said, making my move. "I was hoping I might have a word."

"Of course, of course," he said. "Happy to spare a moment or two. Please, this way."

He headed towards the master suite. I gave Ayesha a glance and an almost imperceptible shrug. She smiled—she was more than happy to play her role with this lot for a few minutes, at least.

"I hope you don't mind my saying it is a bit surprising to see you here," Copta said, ushering me in.

"Well, I hope you don't mind my saying it was a bit of a surprise to get here," I said. "The invite Ayesha received was last minute. Someone had to cancel, but she figured friend-of-a-friend wouldn't be too much of a stretch."

"Well, this boat is a broad church," he said, sitting at the edge of his bed. "Happy to welcome all. Now, then." He leaned back, planting his palms firmly down as leverage. "What can I do for you?"

"It's the case," I said. "I have some follow-up questions."

"Please, go on."

Despite experience, I could feel my teeth grinding a bit from nerves before I jumped in. Copta's lupine charm and confidence might be difficult to navigate—especially considering his history.

"Rumour as it you're helping the police with their investigation?" I asked.

"Absolutely. The Duclos family have been good friends for a long time. This is just terrible about Yannick."

"Mmhmm," I said. I checked out the room. King-sized bed, matched neatly with what was an at least queen-sized, high-def TV on the wall across. A desk with a stack of unopened mail, on top of which lay some colourful envelopes. Invitations, I guessed. One had hearts for an upcoming Valentine's bash, another red postcard featured an ornate crown. In the corner, a couch that looked even softer than the Rolls' back seat leather. There was the expected art—a couple of framed paintings, and a vase that I assumed was worth a lot more than the calla lilies it housed—but nothing overly personal.

"You on this thing a lot?" I asked.

"Oh yes. Love it. Great for entertaining, great for business."

"And the cops—they're interested in what you're offering?"

"Well, I'm offering them access to my books, specifically the work that Yannick did for me. If there's anything there that could give them a lead…" He shrugged. "Well, I'm happy to help. We dealt with a lot of money. Could corrupt anybody I suppose."

I pulled the chair from the desk and sat directly across from Copta.

"These are not going to be nice questions," I said. "But as I am assisting in the investigation, I would appreciate your forthrightness."

"As I said—happy to help."

"Aren't you worried about the police poking into your business?"

"Not particularly, no."

"Even though you are responsible for bringing considerable amounts of heroin into London?"

Copta rocked on his hands a bit, turning his head away. I could still see his smile.

"Welllll," he said, drawing the word out. "That was a long time ago."

"Are you sure the cops will see it that way? And besides, I hear it's possibly still a side hustle for you"

"I'm confident the tracks of the past have long been covered."

"Still, though."

Copta turned his head back to face me, cocking it slightly.

"You think I had something to do with this," he said.

"I don't think anything," I countered. "In this line of work, we just work with theories and trace our steps back."

"Remove the impossible and anything that's left, no matter how improbable, as to the answer? Is that how the saying goes?"

"I think Arthur Conan Doyle made this business sound a lot more interesting than it is," I said. "And I don't smoke a pipe."

"This is quite the accusation, by the way. Even if I have acknowledged its veracity, it's pretty brave to say that to someone."

"I figure a guy like you doesn't scare too easily. So, I gotta ask: Do you know what happened to Duclos?"

He leaned in a bit closer. I could smell what I remembered to be expensive scotch mingling nicely with a subtle cologne.

"I don't know where Mr. Duclos is," he said. "He did a lot of good work for me. He was, by all accounts, a decent man. His family felt like family to me."

"What better way to throw off suspicion than offering help?"

"You cannot be serious."

"Either you—or someone—got rid of him, or, one way or the other, he got rid of himself. And if that's the case, he's going to be a lot harder to find."

"Well then," he said, standing, smoothing the crease of his narrow black trousers. "I guess you'd better get to work."

I put the chair back and joined him heading back to the party.

"How long is this thing?" I asked.

"Over 150 feet."

"Pretty big for one person."

He stopped, and for the first time his appraisal was truly icy. "What do you mean?"

"No wedding ring," I said. "No pics of wife or kids. Looks like it's just you here. And your money, of course."

Ayesha saw us coming round the corner and waved. Unsurprisingly, there were two blandly handsome, gym-fit guys flitting about. I wondered what other stories she had made up to amuse herself in conversation. I waved back.

I shook Copta's hand. He squeezed, tighter than necessary, and jerked me close.

"The fear of being alone is worse than the reality," he said into my ear. "So why don't you and your date get off my boat and enjoy your night somewhere else, hm?"

Something about that had stung him. Copta's manners had faded fast.

"No problem," I said. "Know anywhere good to get a bite around here?"

Copta dropped my hand

"You push your luck," he said, a snarl's edge hiding in the back of his throat.

"Hey, you said to enjoy my night."

"Côte Brasserie," he said. "French place. Pretty good. Try not to choke on it."

21

"So, how'd that go?" Ayesha asked.

We strode briskly down past the water, heading towards Tower Hill Tube station for a lift. Despite Copta's culinary suggestion, I had suggested we not linger in the neighborhood any longer than necessary, and offered to buy her dinner at a decent tapas place I knew around Trafalgar.

"I don't think he had anything to do with it," I said, resignedly.

"But?"

"I do think he is a dangerous man."

"No kidding." Ayesha pulled her wrap a little tighter round herself. It was mild, but the second week of February still offered something of a bite in the air. "The company I had wasn't much more entertaining. Decidedly less threatening, though, I'm sure."

"Other than that, how did you enjoy yourself?" I asked.

She laughed. "You sure know how to show a girl a nice night out, Mr. Grayle."

"Yeah, thanks. I don't hear that as often as you might think."

She nudged me towards a bench near the station, intent to finish our conversation without the rattling of the train barreling through the Underground. She took of her shoes and wiggled her toes.

"Four days," she said.

I squeezed my hands together, leaning forward slightly.

"Yep," was all I said.

"You gonna ask for more time?"

"Nope."

We sat quietly then, watching the people heading in to hop on either the District or Circle lines. I wasn't really a fan of either. Thanks to my flat's location and my inclination for a few jazz clubs, I was mainly a Piccadilly or Victoria guy.

"I don't have the money," she said. "Not handy. I take care of my mother—"

I raised my hand.

"I get it. It's OK. I wouldn't have even asked."

Pause.

"I hope you have a plan," she said.

I let a little air slip through the corner of my mouth.

"I usually find my response to crisis in the moment," I finally said.

"I'd be lying if I said I hadn't hoped this might all wrap itself up on the USS *Gentleman Heroin Smuggler* back there."

"I don't think he would be the roll over and confess his sins type."

"I can be pretty convincing."

"Helps if you have, you know, actual evidence. Knowing he moves H is not the same as him knowing where our missing man is."

"I've never seen a drug dealer so blasé about his job," I said. "I'm kind of impressed."

"So, what's your next move?"

I sat back, looking skyward, but pulling my fingers apart to avoid looking like I was in a state of prayer. I felt pathetic enough.

"Still have to work the wife. And I'm going to go to his office, talk to people who worked with him. My gut says this plays itself out there. You don't quietly amass 4 million pounds without someone knowing what was going on."

"The wife won't roll."

"No, but it's gotta be in the approach. I mean, she might not know anything really about where Yannick is, but it's worth rattling her. Something might shake loose."

"Could be Yannick's buddy Elmore just didn't like her."

"This seems a bit too big for a guy to be just calling out his buddy's wife."

"Did you like all your ex-wife's friends?"

I considered this, likely for the first time.

"She didn't really have any. She wasn't great at it. It was like she could just kind of pretend to care about other people, enough to get through a work party or a night at the pub, at least."

Ayesha looked at me.

"That's the saddest goddamn thing I ever heard," she said.

I shrugged.

"It's like everything else," I said. "Family, jobs, relationships. You don't see those things until you're no longer in the middle of it. I'm sure I had my faults."

"Oh yeah? Like what?"

"Oh, you know. The usual. I was prone to moodiness. Arrogance. An astonishing capacity for alcohol. Chewed my food too loudly. You know—the full gamut, really."

We both laughed a little then, softly, in the dark.

"What about you? You have anybody?" I asked.

She shook her head. "Once. It was pretty serious."

"I get it. You're afraid of commitment."

She shook her head again, a bit slower this time.

"No, not really." She sucked in a bit of air. I realized she wasn't sure if she was going to say anything further.

"It's OK," I said. "None of my business."

"He died," she said.

I let that sit between us for a moment.

"I'm sorry," I said.

"It was a few years ago. Anyhow." She leaned forward, slipping her pumps back on. "All in the past."

"You still up for dinner?"

She shook her head. "Nah. Appetite's shot. Sitting in the dark, feeling sorry for ourselves—imagine how maudlin we'd get over olives and chopitos."

I stood too. We shook hands.

"I'll follow up tomorrow," I said. "Thanks for this."

"Hey, you're footing the bill. Don't sweat it," she said. She wanted to be glib, of course, but her eyes were tender. Kind, even. I gave her forearm a quick pat.

Her phone buzzed. She reached in, opening a text.

"Hunh," she said.

"What's up?"

"It's a guy I know, does a little bookmaking and runs a card game for a lot of people we might have met on that yacht."

"Rich and bored, then."

"Gold star for you, Mr. Teacher," she said. "Anyhow, we go back a bit. I asked him and a few others to keep an eye out for that Raynott kid and his flatmate."

I dug deep, but pulled it up after a second. "Fenske?"

"Yeah. Fenske. Our aspiring tough guy slash dealer. Fenske hit up one of my mate's games. Apparently, he works the room now."

"Seriously? Where'd that guy get that kind of traction?"

"No idea," she said. She held up her phone. "This was the invite. Seen it before?"

I squinted.

On the screen was a crown, five arches and bright red.

Same as was on Duclos' desk.

"Yes," I said, pulling my Oyster card loose and heading towards the station, giving her arm a light tug. She fell into step, matching my pace. "Where's this game happening, then?"

She gave me the details.

"Want to make some overtime?" I asked.

"Sure," she said, pulling her own ticket loose. "If I get my appetite back, you can offer me dinner again, too."

22

Ayesha's source, Max, met us outside. For now, we had the alley to ourselves, but there was no guarantee that would continue. I shuffled my feet, keeping my eyes moving from left to right onto the night street.

"I can't just let you guys in," he said.

"Max," Ayesha said. She reached out, giving his shoulder a playful squeeze, his face a good view of her wide, dark eyes. He was having none of it.

"Ha ha. Nice try. This is high roller time, kid."

"What's the buy in?"

He jerked a thumb towards me.

"Who's the stiff?"

"Hey," I said. "You can talk to me directly, you know."

He ignored me and Ayesha rolled her eyes, mainly to placate Max. Maybe.

"He's cool," she said. "Look, come on. You know we're getting in. We're just negotiating now. What's tonight's buy in?"

He shot me another look, then turned to face Ayesha.

"Five thousand."

"Wow, Max," she said, impressed. "Moving up in the world, hunh?"

"I do OK."

"No kidding. Last time we ran together, you were fencing laptops and mid-range jewelry."

"I'm saving up. Gotta get on the property ladder. Invest in my future."

"You ever see this guy?" I said, showing him a pic of Duclos on my phone.

He didn't even look at it.

"Ayesha, I gotta get back to work. Great seeing you. Give

me a call sometime, yeah? We'll catch up proper."

He turned, but Ayesha grabbed his arm.

"Max," she said. "C'mon. Look at the picture."

"I'm not looking to stitch up any of my players. The people who play here enjoy their anonymity."

"This guy is missing," I said. "We know he played here. We're trying to find him for his wife. And his kid."

Max looked at the picture, then shrugged.

"Max," Ayesha said, her voice low as a prowler. "We need to get inside and meet some of these guys. For all we know, he's in there right now, burning through his son's inheritance."

"He's not in there."

"So you know him?" she asked.

"Yeah," he said. "Yeah, fine, OK? Your man's Yannick D. Comes in about once a month."

"When was the last time he played?" she asked, voice still low and cool, none too fussed. I could feel my own heart stating to pick up a bit, the RPMs building.

"Two weeks ago."

Ayesha and I exchanged a look. I nodded.

"We need to get inside," she said. "What's it going to take?"

"What, besides five grand? Not much."

"OK, how about this: You let us in, and spot us the money," she said.

Max reacted predictably, but Ayesha cut him off in mid-snort.

"Max, you let us in, and give us money to get in. We aren't going to play much. We just need some info. You get it all back. But we need cover. You do that. And I'll tell you what I know about when you got rumbled by the cops back in '16."

"Nothing to know. Seller got sloppy and the cops tracked the stuff."

"It was a smash and grab, right? You had to move the jewels fast. How'd the cops find it that quick, though?"

Max was trying to pull a look somewhere between bored and non-committal, but he was lagging.

"You want know who sold you out?" she asked.

Max flashed his teeth, the whites pressed tight against each other here in the alley's lone lightbulb's glare.

"This better be on the up-and-up," he said through that savage smile.

She nodded. "It is. Want the name?"

"Yes," he said, the 's' spaced out in a hiss.

"J-Block. Guy who did some driving for you."

"What, that kid? He wouldn't dare."

"He got picked up on a warrant. Rolled on you to get loose. Remember he wasn't around for a while?"

"Nah," Max said. "Nah. He was solid."

"Well, I guess you'll just have to ask him," she said, opening her phone and showing him a number. "Maybe you give him a call tomorrow. Ask him out for a proper catch up, yeah?"

Max smiled in spite of himself.

"You better be telling me the truth," he said, turning towards the door. Ayehsa shot me a *c'mon* look and I quickly stepped to it.

"It's golden, trust me," she said.

"Why didn't you tell me this before?" he asked. We were in a closed Chinese restaurant's kitchen. He headed to a door in the back, leading towards the cellar.

"We haven't seen each other in a while," she said. "Besides, it's always best to say less than you know. Keeps people guessing."

We came to the bottom of the stairs. Max banged on the iron-wrought door ahead with two hard thumps, then another. A latch clattered from behind.

"Cute," he said to Ayesha as the door opened. "You'll need a better poker face than that tonight. These guys aren't messing."

"This the part we we're supposed to say, 'Neither are we'?" I asked.

Max sighed.

"Yeah, sure. If it were true," he said. We stepped inside.

23

"You know what you're doing?" I asked. It was more a hopeful observation than a straight-up question. Ayesha was calmly counting out two stacks of chips as I drummed my fingers on the bartop.

"Oh yeah. I played a lot." She checked one of the pillars against some loose chips in her hand. "Back in the old days."

I was going to make a crack about how her old days were maybe three weeks ago, but then recalled Ayehsa had likely seen some of the heaviest shit anyone under 30 has a right to endure. I instead decided to wisely keep my mouth shut.

"You see Fenske?" I asked.

She shook her head.

"OK. I'm hanging here. If you see him, let me know."

She looked up from her chips.

"How?" she asked. "It's not like I'm allowed to use my phone out there."

"I dunno, you're the, ah, physical presence in this working relationship. Improvise."

"Wait—*I'm* the muscle?" she asked, mock incredulously.

"God, yes. I get to be the brains of the outfit."

"Don't strain your neck with your head getting so big."

"Don't waste time with banter when your table and possible wealth of intel awaits," I said. A brief eye-roll later, she made her way to a game. I waved to the barman and got a Coke.

Ayesha's description of Fenske—short, thin, long-ish sandy hair, face featuring a few lingering acne craters—would certainly mark him out here. The average age was mid-50s and the look decidedly clean-cut. By any reckoning, this was a pro operation. Hands were dealt quickly, and the only chatter was the occasional exchange of peasantries between returning players. There were at least two heavies strategically positioned in opposite corners, keeping an eye on the tables and the players, their presence meant as a reminder to play nice. Nothing I saw suggested anyone had other intentions.

"How's your night?" I asked the bartender, an older guy with neatly trimmed pewter stubble and a decent head of greying hair. He ignored me, tending to his cleaning duties.

"Great to hear," I muttered.

He continued wiping down glasses as I took in the room, trying to scan without looking too obvious. Ayesha was getting dealt in. We would have to be quick—her bravado aside, we couldn't risk losing too much of that pile.

"Fenske works in the cash room," I heard over my shoulder. I turned. The barman was stacking dried tumblers in a rack and hadn't moved, but he had certainly spoken.

"How's that?" I asked.

He began slicing limes and did not raise his head to face me.

"Fenske's in back," he said, his lips barely moving. I took his cue and turned away, back to the pit.

"How do I get to him?" I asked, rubbing my chin to hide my mouth.

"Fifty quid," he murmured.

I nodded, slipping the crisp bill under my now-empty glass. Satisfied, the barman continued.

"He takes his break in a few. Usually hits the head before going out for a smoke." From my peripheral, I traced his eye line to the WASHROOMS sign in the room's rear.

"Thanks," I said, voice low. I pushed the glass towards him. He scooped both it and the money up in one smooth motion.

"No problem," he said. "Fenske stiffed me on my share of the table tips last week." He switched to lemons. "Have fun."

I smothered my smile and kept an eye on the gents. Several minutes later, a skinny kid with bad skin walked into the washroom. I headed over.

For a kid working in a decidedly upscale—if illegal—operation, Fenske hadn't really done himself a lot of favours, appearance-wise. His trainers were scuffed and his shirt, a baggy flannel number, hung low and untucked. I closed the door behind me as he approached the sink to wash his hands.

"Evening," I said.

He gave a barely-perceptible nod.

"Busy tonight?" I continued.

He shrugged. "Bit, yeah. You playing?"

I shook my head. "Just here with a friend."

He dried his fingers on some crinkly brown paper towel.

"Well, have a good night," he said, already bored with our chit-chat.

I didn't move, blocking his path to the door.

"Hey," he said, taking a step back.

"We need to talk," I said. I held up the picture of Duclos.

He groaned. "C'mon, man." He shot a nervous glance to the two stalls.

"No one's here but us," I said. "I watched before coming in. So: let's talk."

"About what?" he said, trying to work his voice up to a snarl.

"About you moving heroin, for starters," I said. "Pretty sure the authorities would enjoy a tip about your day job."

He took this in. I kept my eyes on his hands. Guys working the cash in a place like this probably weren't allowed to carry their own weapons around, but you never knew.

"The guys here don't know I deal," he finally said. "I'm finished if they find out."

"Well, then. Let's make sure they don't."

I wasn't going to get rough with Fenske—it was not really my style—but he didn't know that. Truth be told, for a drug dealer and aspiring member of London's criminal underworld, he was a bit underwhelming, physically. I might be able to simply sweat him out. That was the hope. Confidence was, as always, key.

"Look, kid, it's option A or option B," I said, my voice edged between bored and threatening. "Real simple. So let's have it."

Hs eyes darted from the picture and back to me.

"You know who runs this game?" he asked.

I shook my head.

"Albanians," he said. "Heavy hitters. Your guy there" — he nodded to the pic — "he liked to play. He was good, too. Head for numbers, they said."

"So I've heard."

"Anyhow, he had a few big wins. Gets a sit-down with one of the bosses, mid-level guy. He thinks he's in shit or something."

"He wasn't?"

Fenske shook his head. "Nah, guy didn't cheat. He played the percentages, sure, but he was also good. Tough to read at the table. He earned his money, far as I could tell."

"So what'd they want with him?"

"I don't know," Fenske said, his voice getting little higher. He was starting to panic, probably worried about being away for too long.

"Settle down," I said. "You seen him since?"

Fenske shook his head again, a bit more pace to it this time.

"Can you find out what that chat was about?" I pressed.

"I think I'd rather go to jail for dealing heroin," he said, and I think he meant it.

I sighed and stepped aside. He pulled the door in with a jerk, shooting me a look dirty as I'd seen in a while.

"Thanks for the help," I said, with more than a little good cheer.

"Yeah, sure," he said stepping out. "Asshole."

I shrugged as the door swung shut. *Fair enough.* I waited a minute, then followed him out.

Ayesha's stack was, thank God, pretty much unchanged as I ambled back to the bar. The barman showed no sign of recognition, but I hoped Fenske's distress as he crossed the floor offered him some pleasure. I shot Ash a look and she nodded.

"Aw, c'mon" the player to her left said, a pudgy guy with a heavy gold bracelet rattling around a thick wrist. "Stick around."

"Sorry, gents," she said, scooping up her stake. "Ladies night is over. Another time."

We headed back to the front door to exchange her chips.

"Get everything?" she asked, sliding them over.

"Yeah," I said. "Everything I could, I'm pretty sure. How'd you do?"

"Folded a few times, won one hand on a pair of kings," she said. "Came out a couple hundred ahead. I'll leave it for Max. Might keep him out of trouble for a bit."

"I'm thinking it'll take more than that to set him on a righteous path."

"He hurt your feelings," she said, a knowing smirk crossing her face. "You're a big boy. You'll be OK."

24

Later, in the office. I usually kept a bag of ice in the mini-fridge and wrapped some of it in a towel, pressing against my abdomen. It had still been acting up a bit following the pounding it took at The Empress courtesy Quigley's guy. I had sent Ayesha home—that had been enough cloak and dagger for one night and I could use an hour or so to myself. In front of me was a box of Yannick Duclos' personal effects that I had requested be couriered over. A pocket watch from his father. A few old school yearbooks. A stack of glossy snapshots from college parties and friends' weddings. A mix CD Annie had made for him, presumably early in their courtship. I slipped it into my laptop and the machine came alive, struggling to fill the room with its tinny speakers. Wherever Yannick Duclos was, it was unlikely mid-90s college rock and assorted one-hit wonders were going to be the clues that pointed the way—but it helped pass the time.

I was putting on some coffee and weighing my options when my phone buzzed. It was Calloway.

"Hey," I said. "What's up? Enjoying a quiet night in with the opera?"

"It's good, thank you," he said, and right away I could hear it: his cop voice. Clipped, short, no nonsense and banter-free. I slid the mug in place as the java perked, listening to the water's hiss.

"What's going on?" I asked.

"Annie Duclos was found dead in her home tonight."

I tapped my spoon against the machine, letting that wave crash against me.

"Damn it," I managed after a moment. "What happened?"

"Shot. Back of the head, small caliber, close range. She was found at home, in the kitchen."

"Who found her?"

Calloway paused.

"The kid," he said after a moment.

I closed my eyes. We were silent for a second.

"Yeah, I know," he finally said.

"How is he?"

"Not great." I could hear the click of a lighter and Calloway's intake of breath. Not all his vices had been abandoned.

"Thanks for the heads up," I said.

"Thought you'd like to know. Get ahead of it a bit."

I poured myself a cup.

"Ahead of what?" I asked.

"I imagine you're going to get asked about this. You were in contact with Annie professionally and you were digging deep into the life of a man who is either dead himself or on the run. Stranger things have happened."

"What, stranger than me killing my client?"

"Don't get defensive. It's procedure. You've got an alibi, right?"

I took a deep slug from the cup. Too strong. I always made it too strong. I never got used to making it myself.

"Yeah," I said. "Yeah, I'm good."

"Then I advise you get down to the scene and talk to Dunsmore. She's there right now, working the scene."

There was a small washroom off to side of my office. I dumped the ice into the sink and re-tucked my shirt, wincing only briefly.

"Guess she got her wish," I said. "Climbing the ladder, I mean."

"Yeah, well, it's a helluva way to get to work a homicide," Calloway said. "But between you and her, you both know more about this family than anyone. So get down there and offer a helping hand. Make yourself useful."

I slipped on my jacket, buttoning it gingerly in front of my stomach.

"You there?" he asked, only a few decibels short of a bark. "You gotta move now if you want to have any say in how this plays out."

I looked at the box on my desk, a cardboard cask holding a few lingering shadows of a man who might have well been a ghost—and a wife who now was.

"Who's with the kid?" I asked.

"Don't know."

I grabbed my keys. "OK. I'm heading out."

"Don't spare the whip. I know one of the uniforms down there. I'll text, let her know you're coming."

"Calloway," I said, taking the stairs two at a time as I plunged down the stairwell to my Saab. "Thanks, man. Owe ya one."

"Help Dunsmore and we'll call it square," he said as I crossed the alley, stabbing my door with the key and slipping inside. "She's good police. Don't piss her off."

My car growled to life. I toed the accelerator and slipped out into the Shoreditch night. The fog hung low.

"That was not my intention," I said.

"Good. Glad to hear," he said. "And for God's sake—do something to help find out what the hell is going on with this family."

25

I got to the Duclos house in about 30 minutes, occupying myself with impatient radio station changes and a half-empty and well-warm bottle of Diet Coke stowed under the seat. When I arrived, the street was lit in red and blue lights, but silent except for a few people gathered on the walk outside, gawkers trying to get their first cherished strands of gossip elbow-to-elbow with a couple of genuinely worried neighbours. I politely walked by them before being greeted by a uniformed officer's upturned palm.

"Hold up," she said. "You Grayle?"

I nodded. She leaned her head close to her shoulder walkie, which gave a short squawk. I couldn't hear the exchange, but apparently I had passed muster. She waved me under towards the door.

Inside, a few more uniforms milled about, and a photographer, lanyard tucked carefully inside his windbreaker, crouched low to the floor. I could see Annie Duclos' feet jutting out from behind the kitchen island. One shoe, a slightly battered ballet flat, had been knocked loose as she hit the tiles, and now hung, askew, off her left toes. Dunsmore was in hushed chat with another officer, and headed my way.

"Grayle," she said. "We were just about to get in touch."

"Had a feeling," I said. "Thought I'd come in myself, offer anything you guys might need by way of help."

The cop Dunsmore had been talking to heard this, and cocked his head. Dunsmore took me by the arm and pulled me deeper into the living room.

"What do you have?" she asked.

"Where's the kid?" I asked.

She paused, a brief quizzical look crossing her face.

"What?"

"The kid," I answered. "Aiden."

"He's in his room."

"Can I have a word?"

Dunsmore rolled her linebacker shoulders a bit, trying to loosen them up. I guessed she had already been up a few more hours than expected.

"Sure," she said. "Why not." She pointed down the hall. I walked through the kitchen, keeping my gaze straight as I passed Annie.

There was a young officer in the room, standing by the door, clearly uncomfortable. I nodded as I entered. Relieved, he took that as his sign to step back outside.

Aiden was sitting at his desk, still in his school uniform, the note pad in front of him accompanied by a can of ginger ale, its straw sticking straight up. There was no other chair, so I sat on the edge of the bed. He didn't acknowledge me. I waited for a few moments. I had learned this long ago, thanks to the husbands or wives walking into my office, waiting for the bad news they knew was coming. When you walk into a room like this, heavy with the jolt and fog of catastrophic news, you need to let the charge in the air die down a bit.

Aiden had his pen over the paper, but it wasn't moving.

"Hey," I said.

He said nothing, just gave a short nod of recognition.

"What are you working on?" I asked.

He shrugged.

"Nothing. Homework. It's stupid."

"I used to be a teacher," I said. "I almost never assigned homework. I hated marking it."

"Guess you were a pretty popular teacher, then," he said. He still hadn't looked up my way.

I waited another minute or so.

"Did you speak to the police?" I asked.

He nodded.

"What'd they say?"

"They're trying to track down my mum's sister. She lives in Spain."

"Do you need anything?"

111

He shook his head then took a sip from the ginger ale's straw.

"Where were you today? Before you got home?"

He shrugged again.

"Nowhere. Walking around. Hanging out." He dipped his head towards a plastic bag near the head of the bed. I looked inside. It was the rule book for some fantasy role-playing game, the cover adorned with a gleaming-armoured knight and spell-summoning mage, both facing off against a scaled red dragon looking to turn them to ash.

"Some of the kids at school play," he said. "There's a club."

"Yeah, I used to play stuff like this," I said.

"What was your character?" he asked.

"Um," I said. "Which time? I played a lot."

He didn't quite smile, but his lips flattened a little.

"My first ever character was a rogue," I said. "You know, one of those sneaky guys who can pick locks and hide in shadows."

"Maybe that's why you do your job," he said.

Hunh. "Maybe. I had never thought of that. What are you looking to play?"

"I like the guys with the bows, the rangers. Maybe a paladin. I dunno."

"Paladin? Like those holy warrior knights?"

He nodded.

"Yeah, you can play them so they're like on this quest," he said. "Or maybe avenging something."

I crossed my legs, shaking one out a bit. It had fallen asleep. I scanned the book shelf above his headboard. Mostly graphic novels and a few sci fi paperbacks—some Asimov, a battered Phillip K. Dick.

I stood.

"Hey," I said. I laid one of my cards in front of him, on top of the lined notepaper. It was blank.

He looked up. His eyes were red, their veins cracked and the skin around them dark and puffy. But they were dry now.

"You want to talk, you can call or text me," I said.

"Thanks," he mumbled.

I tapped the open book.

"I don't think they're going to be checking your homework tomorrow, Aiden."

He nodded.

"Try and get some rest," I said.

I walked out, the last thing I saw before I turned by the door was him laying his forehead on the lip of his desk. I hesitated briefly, and kept walking.

Dunsmore was waiting for me in the hall.

"Well?" she asked.

I stopped.

"I'm sorry, I don't understand," I said.

"What'd he say?"

"I didn't really ask him anything."

She clicked her jaw.

"So why were you in there?"

"I'm just checking that he was OK," I said. "Where are you putting him tonight?"

"Hotel," she said. "We'll have someone from the Council in tomorrow."

"Any luck with finding the sister?"

"We're still trying to get her on the phone," she said.

"Any leads on the shooting?"

"Yeah. One or two," she said. She reached into her jacket and pulled out a piece of nicotine gum, unwrapping it before popping it into her mouth for a few aggressive chews. She pulled out her notebook.

"What about you?" she asked. "Any ideas?"

"You wanna talk here?"

"Why? You want to go to Westminster?"

"Not particularly," I said. "I met the kid once during my preliminary investigation of the missing husband. Nothing suggested threats of violence to the family, either through him or my conversations with Annie Duclos."

"Who else you talk to?"

"The usual," I said. "Friends. Both current and former. Colleagues. And your new friend Copta."

She looked up from her notes. "He has been assisting in the

investigation, yes."

"You know his background?"

She nodded. "This is a homicide, not a long-over narcotics investigation."

One of the uniforms asked Dunsmore if she wanted a coffee. She nodded and gave me a look.

"Sure," I shrugged. "Thanks. So you don't like Copta for this?"

"Not yet," she said. "Bit weird that he'd kill Annie when he was in the middle of making himself available to us for questioning related to her husband's disappearance."

"You'd have to admit that all of this is pretty goddamned weird, Dunsmore," I said.

She sighed, one of weariness rather than frustration.

"Yeah," she said. "No kidding. Hell of a way to work a first murder."

"They sending in anyone else?"

"Yeah, a DI who is in Homicide proper. He's on his way. I'm just getting the ball rolling here."

She flipped to a fresh page.

"So," she said. "Where were you earlier?"

"If you don't fancy Copta for this you must be mad to think I had anything to do with it."

"Don't be so dramatic," she said. "It's protocol. So let's go."

"I was on Copta's yacht earlier tonight. After which my colleague, Ayesha Gill, and I attended an underground card game as part of my investigation into the missing Duclos."

Dunsmore looked up. "Seriously?"

I nodded.

"And someone there will back that up?"

"Yeah. Plenty of people on the yacht. And my associate will vouch for the rest."

"OK. Make sure we get some names and numbers."

"First thing tomorrow."

The uniform came in, back from his errand and handing us our coffees.

"Anything else I should know?" Dunsmore asked.

"Well, uh, yes," I said.

"Cream?" the uniform asked. I shook my head, Dunsmore grabbed a little tub and dumped it in.

"Like what?" she asked.

I took a sip.

"Um. Well, Duclos had a significant gambling habit and I'm guessing regularly hit up some pretty rough joints, one of which has ties to the Albanian mafia. That's where I spent my night. He also had accumulated about 4 million pounds in cash over the last few years, all of which was cleaned through various clients and shell companies and is now hidden in several Swiss accounts."

After a painfully long moment, Dunsmore handed her coffee to the officer who brought them. He took it without a word or making eye contact with his superior. She slowly opened her notebook and poised her pen above it.

I glanced over at the uniform and raised my cup. "Sorry, mate—thanks, by the way."

Dunsmore bared her teeth.

"Anything else?" she asked, her voice like a tire rolling slowly over gravel.

I nodded.

"Yeah. Annie Duclos is the only person who knew of the existence of these accounts, and even she didn't have the passwords. So…"

I let my voice trail off.

Dunsmore snapped her notebook shut and grabbed her coffee back.

"So: that money is gone," she said. "Duclos is gone, the wife is gone in the most real sense of the word, and that money is, for all intents and purposes, gone. That's what 'so' means, is it, Grayle?"

"I probably could have delivered this all a bit better," I said.

"Yeah," she said. "No shit." She barked at another officer who hurried over. Pointing at me, she said, "Get him out of here. Get him home."

"I drove," I said.

"That's great," she snapped. "Bully for you. Get home safe.

You're coming in tomorrow morning, 8 a.m., for a chat. Try not to bury the lede this time, Grayle."

26

Back at my flat. I had been trying to settle down and get some sleep but my mind wouldn't stop pinwheeling. I hopped off the couch and began playing with my long-neglected turntable, finally laying down some Herbie Hancock. The noise swelled, warm and true, in the darkness of the flat. I grabbed a Diet Coke and plopped on the couch, flipping channels in the dark, the TV on mute.

My phone hummed. It was Ayesha.

"Yeah?" I asked.

"Let me in. Got those files for you."

I took a drag from the can.

"This isn't a great time."

"Then don't look at them. But if you think I'm lugging these things around for kicks, you're mad."

If nothing else, she could always be counted on for both her work efficiency and conversational economy. I buzzed her in.

"Got anything to drink?" she asked. In one hand was a small takeaway bag and, in the other, a folder thick as a phone book. She laid the file down and headed for the kitchen.

"Soda's in the fridge. Kettle is on the counter if you fancy some tea."

I heard her clinking about the refrigerator.

"I know you don't drink, but surely some of your guests might fancy a beer every now and then," she said, emerging

"Y'know, it's not yet come up," I said.

She sat across from me, setting up her drink and sandwich, tugging her phone loose from her jacket.

"Why *don't* you drink?" she asked.

"Why don't you ever cook for yourself?" I replied, nodding to her takeaway.

"Thad," she said, slipping her straw from its paper.

"C'mon."

I shrugged. "Dunno. I'm better without it."

"Do you miss it?"

"Sometimes, yeah," I said. I stretched out a bit. "But it's not a big deal."

"So you just stopped?"

I nodded.

"Something trigger that decision?"

"Sure. Busted marriage. Career ennui. General depression and loneliness. I was gaining a bit of weight. You know—the usual."

"You look good, you feel good."

"I don't know about good, but definitely better," I said. "So: can we get to work now?"

"Long as I'm here," she said, popping the lid on her cola. "I can give you the quick version of what our guy found in the financials."

"Anything that's going to blow the thing wide open?" I asked. "Like, say, a roadmap to wherever the hell this guy is?"

She shook her head.

"Then it'll keep 'til tomorrow," I said. "Just e-mail me the CliffsNotes later."

She nodded, tucking enthusiastically into her sarnie.

"You going to ask me how my night was?" I said.

She looked up, giving me *go on* eyes as she chewed.

I sighed, heading over to the turntable and flipping Herbie's *Maiden Voyage* over to side two.

"Annie Duclos is dead," I said. "Shot in the head in her kitchen."

She sat back a bit.

"No shit," she said, after a moment. "Wow."

"Yeah."

I sat back down. She too another bite of the sandwich. Ham and cheese, by the look of it.

"Cops call you?" she asked.

"Sort of," I said. "I got a buddy in Professional Standards. He gave me a heads up. I met with the team at the scene."

"They figure you for it?"

"Nope. But they're bringing me in for questioning tomorrow morning."

"Why's that?"

I resisted the urge to bite my bottom lip, instead momentarily focusing my gaze on the rim of the LP slowly spinning across the room.

"I told them everything we knew about Duclos."

She put the sandwich down.

"Oh god damn it," she said.

I nodded.

"Thad—"

"What else could I do?" I asked. "It's a *homicide*."

"Do you have anything to give them?"

I nodded towards a stack of notes on piled next to my TV.

"Just the interviews with who we spoke with, all of which were completely unilluminating in their own way. Plus, whatever your accountant friend dug loose from all the financial records, which of course the cops already have themselves and so probably know even more than we do."

"What about the money? *Your* money?"

I over-shrugged, an attempt to signal my frustration. Instead, I only managed to trigger a twinge in my still-bruised solar plexus—a reminder of what awaited.

"So what's the next move?" she asked.

I pressed the heels of my hands into my eyes. Hard.

"Thad," she said.

I stood up and headed to the fridge, grabbing another Coke.

"I think there's still some left in that one," she said. "Sounded pretty full when you laid it down."

"Maybe *you* should be the detective," I said, falling back onto the couch, grabbing my TV remote.

She took that in for a second.

"OK," she said, standing. She gathered her stuff. I jabbed the buttons on the remote, settling on Channel 4.

"I know you're smart enough to realize the seriousness of this," she said. "But I also know you are a stubborn, stubborn man."

"I'm not following you," I said, propping a pillow behind

119

my head as I leaned back.

"Well, you could always ask your ex-wife for the money," she said at the door.

I didn't respond.

"'Cause she's, you know. Rich."

"Her husband is rich," I said, evenly.

"You worked enough divorce cases," she said. "You know it's all 50-50, right?"

I stretched out a bit further and re-angled the pillow underneath my head.

"Make sure you pull the door closed behind you," I said. "Sticks sometimes."

"Sure," she said. She buckled her coat's belt and stepped through the frame. "But you might want to climb down from that woe-is-me cross sooner than later. 'Cause the last two times I've come here there's the same guy in the same car outside, parked in front of the grocer's."

I looked over.

"Red hair, pulled back in a ponytail. Looks pretty Irish," she said. "But what do I know, right? I'm not the detective."

She left, with not another word. I changed the channel.

27

If Dunsmore had cooled down any from our conversation last night, she certainly wasn't letting on. She greeted me with the curtest of nods as she settled into the chair across from me. She nodded to her colleague, who introduced himself as DI Bronson Moore, Homicide division.

"Nice to meet you," I said.

"It's early," he said, with genuine joviality. "You might change your mind."

I tried to make eye contact with Dunsmore, give her the *Are you guys gonna really pull this cop stuff* look, but she was busying herself with the folder.

"How's Aiden?" I asked.

"Managing," Moore replied.

"Can't hope for much more, I suppose," I said.

"Mr. Grayle," Moore said. He reached over to press record on a large black box that sat off to the left. "We will be recording this conversation. I will begin—"

He rattled off his and Dunsore's names, badge numbers and the time and date. He looked at me. I gave him my full name and home address.

"And your occupation, for the record?"

"Seriously?" I asked.

"For the record," he said, a little slower, as if the problem was my cognitive ability.

"I'm a private investigator."

"How long have you been one?"

"Um. About five years."

"And your specialty is infidelity and divorce cases, correct?"

"It was, yeah. But I don't work those anymore. I've branched out a bit."

"What changed?"

"Professional aspirations, I suppose."

"Which neatly explains how you got hired by Annie Duclos to find her missing husband."

"That's the logical conclusion, yes."

He made some notes on the pad in front of him. I tried again to meet Dunsmore's eyes and finally succeeded. But they were flat. Unmoved. I sighed inwardly.

"Do you know where Yannick Duclos is?" Moore asked.

"No."

"Do you know who killed Annie Duclos?"

I leaned my chair back, rocking on its hind legs a bit.

"C'mon, guys," I said. "My alibi checks out. What are you looking for here?"

"How can you be so naïve?" Dunsmore said, her voice low but strong. They were the first words to escape her mouth since I had arrived.

"What? What's that supposed to mean?"

"You hid information from us in the course of an investigation." She was angry—I could tell by the slight stretch to her neck's tendons—but was doing a good job controlling it. I imagined I was not the first man in this chair to disappoint her. "Did you not think it might have been, I dunno, *germane*, to come clean a bit before this?"

"Hold up," I said. "You told me that this wasn't even a big priority for the cops, that guys like Duclos run off all the time. *I* was just doing my job. Like you, but, you know, with something resembling a sense of urgency."

"And how'd that go?" she snapped back. "Did that urgency get you anywhere closer to finding him, right before Annie Duclos got shot in the back of her skull?" She opened the folder in front of her. The full report of Annie's death was there, plus several photos of Annie's corpse. One close-up showed her right profile, the eye still open and staring up at her ceiling. Her head lay in a shallow pool of blood, whose spread had been stopped only by the click of the camera's shutter.

I slowly lowered my seat back to the floor.

Moore cleared his throat.

"Tell us about the money," he said.

I gave them everything I knew. They scribbled furiously away. Dunsmore even checked the machine to make sure it was all getting on tape. When I was done, Moore tapped a pen against his now well-worn pad.

"$4 million," he muttered. "Cripes."

"I know," I said. "Smart guy."

We sat in silence for a moment.

"Any leads on the shooting?" I asked. "No forced entry, right? Someone she knew?"

Moore and Dunsmore looked at each other.

"I think we're done here," Moore said, standing.

"Guys," I said. "C'mon."

Dunsmore shrugged. Moore packed his notes in a slim briefcase.

"Thank you for your time, Mr. Grayle," he said. He didn't even look at me as he walked out, closing the door behind him.

"That your new boss?" I asked.

"Maybe," she said. She leaned over, turning off the machine. "Depends how this investigation goes and if I get a chance to join homicide."

"What he lacks in manners he apparently more than makes up for in paperwork," I said. "So you'll have fun, at least."

Dunsmore wasn't smiling. We weren't close to being there yet, and I should have known that.

"Sorry if I threw you under the bus a bit with the 'lack of urgency' thing," I said.

"No, no, that was great, thank you," she said. "Who wouldn't enjoy seeing themselves being slapped down by a grubby little snoop in front of the man who controls their professional future?"

"Hey, don't spare my feelings."

She began packing up her own things. The file spilled out. I stooped under the table to grab some and hand it to her. She grabbed it, a little roughly.

"Felicity," I said. Her face turned to mine, eyes flashing.

I took a breath, slowly, trying to make sure it didn't sound like a weary sigh.

"I'm sorry, OK?" I said. "But it's my job. Same as yours."

"It is not the same as mine," she snapped. "You think I'm an idiot? You think *he's* an idiot? The Duclos woman had no money. None. We know everything about their financials. So unless you were doing this out of the goodness of your heart, you were going to get paid with some of that money."

"Assuming you are in any way right," I said. "Not all of it was dirty money, DI Dunsmore."

She rolled her eyes then, deftly and deeply.

"Look, I'm in trouble here too," I said. "And there's a lot more on the line than a pat on the back from my boss."

"The perils of being your own employer, I guess," she said. "Show you out?"

We fell into stride down the hall. The building clamored: phones bleating, leather soles slapping linoleum, voices ringing out.

"Busy, busy," I said.

"I'm sure you'd love it for me to say something self-congratulatory about the never-ending nature of police work, but I'll pass."

She stopped and jerked her head towards the front entrance. I was dismissed.

"Thanks for coming in." She turned to walk away.

"Dunsmore," I said. "The kid. You find that sister yet?"

She stopped, turning around.

"No. But we know she's in Spain. We've contacted the local authorities."

"Why Spain?" I asked.

She sighed.

"Duclos owned a villa there," she said. "It's on his books. We found it this morning. It's all we got."

"Not much of a lead," I said.

"Well. I'm sure you would have found it. Eventually."

"I haven't gotten to the spreadsheets yet," I said. "But I got 'em."

"Of course," she said, smiling thinly.

I nodded good bye sullenly and headed out.

"Who knows, Grayle?" she called after me. "Maybe we'll get really lucky and Yannick Duclos is there, too—enjoying a siesta, blissfully unaware of all this hell that's broken loose back here."

"He'd be better off staying," I said, stepping into the mid-day sun. She didn't have a quick enough answer for that— the door was already shut behind me.

28

I left New Scotland Yard and headed towards Westminster station, dialing Ayesha as I hustled down Embankment, weaving between impatient tourists taking pics with the Eye or Parliament behind them.

"Yeah?" she said.

"Hey," I said. "Still mad?"

"Better believe it."

"Want to know how my interview went?"

"Well, I can hear you're outside, so I guess they didn't find a reason to arrest you."

"True enough. But something came up. Thought you'd like to know about it since it could mean some work. Maybe even a little action."

The line was quiet, but only for a moment.

"I'm listening," she said.

"The cops had the full report on Annie Duclos death in front of me. It had everything about the case, including her full details. Date of birth, list of previous addresses, and her full name."

"So? That's pretty standard, I'm guessing."

"Annie's name was Annabelle Vivian Duclos, nee Ramsey."

"Again: So?"

I was at the station. I popped into Café Nero for a quick caffeine lift and to catch my breath.

"Copta's yacht. It was called *Vivian*."

Another pause.

"And he said he had just gotten it about a year ago," she said.

"Bragged, really. But yeah. About a year."

"Which is when the kid started acting out a bit."

"Mmm hmmm."

I heard her suck some air between her teeth.

"God damn," she finally murmured.

"Could be nothing." I said.

"Listen to your voice. You don't think that for a second."

I mouthed a quick *thank you* to the girl behind the counter and headed towards the turnstiles.

"No," I replied. "I guess I don't. It's a pretty weird coincidence."

"So, what do you think? Copta and her were having an affair?"

"Maybe, yeah. Maybe Yannick finds out and runs off, cleaning them out."

"Or Copta was jealous and had *him* taken out. Maybe Copta's sitting on the money, waiting for this to all blow over."

"Lotta maybes," I said, sliding my Oyster card and picking up the pace towards the Jubilee line. "Wanna go get some definites?"

I could already hear the rustling on the other end. If she wasn't already dressed, she was well on her way.

"I'll see you at your office," she said.

"Already on way," I said. "You can bring two sandwiches this time, if you're picking something up."

About ten minutes later, I was bounding up the stairs at Liverpool Street Station, pulling my phone loose as I ducked around the corner. That, and my unchecked enthusiasm, had left me a little sloppy, exposed, so I didn't see the flash to my left until a split-second too late. The fist came in hard and fast, but controlled—there was no energy wasted, nothing more expended than what was felt to be necessary. I dropped immediately to my knees, in time for the next blow—again, short, tight, like a crossbow string snapping off a bolt—to catch me on the right cheek, just above my lip.

The guy was a pro. He had angled me back into the alley and used his frame to block any view of me from the street. The morning rush hour crowd would never even think to cast us a sideways glance.

I still couldn't breathe. My hands propped me up, but I was still on my knees, crab-like and defenseless. He roughly hooked his arm under mine and pulled me up. He had pale skin, and a healthy shock of red hair, tied back in a loose ponytail.

"Morning," he said.

"Chrissakes," I barely managed. Clean shot to the solar plexus. Again. It hurt to talk. Any air both coming in and out of my body was bringing a lot of complications to me, pain-wise. "What's the *matter* with you guys? I still got a couple days."

"Mr. Quigley wants you to know understand the seriousness of this deal," Ponytail said. "We have heard you are encountering difficulties making ends meet."

"The hell…?" I asked.

He shrugged. I finally twigged it.

"The Met," I said. "Of course. You got a few cops running errands?"

He nodded.

"Your interview with the police did not go well. We are following up."

I leaned against the wall behind me, enjoying the coolness of the stone as it worked its way through my suit jacket and sweat-drenched shirt.

"Well, you don't waste time, I'll give you that," I said. "I got a lead. Tell Alphonse it's coming together."

"Good," he said. He reached out, placing his hands and their overly-ringed fingers firmly on my shoulders. "Mr. Quigley intends to keep his end of the bargain if you keep yours."

"Pay up or get a kicking," I said. "Pretty standard arrangement, Patty. I get it."

He gave my rapidly-swelling cheek a very gentle—yet very menacing—tap.

"My name's Sean," he said. "And the way we've heard it, some people don't think you care about getting a kicking." He gave my coat front a snap, straightening it out a bit. "And just so you know, it doesn't matter to me if you pay up or not. I make a living either way."

I braced for a parting blow, but he simply pushed off from

my shoulders and walked away. I waited until he turned the corner before allowing myself to slide down the wall, holding my stomach, squeezing my eyes hard until the tears would no longer threaten to spill.

29

Ayesha was in the foyer at my building when I arrived, and I caught a glimpse of a slight smile on her face—evidently, she had forgiven me. I tried to hang onto that memory when she turned, saw me and that smile vanished.

"Jesus, Thad," she said. "You all right?"

I nodded. My stomach was still a mess. Trying to buy a little time, I worked the key into my mailbox.

"Alphonse Quigley has formally sent his regards."

"I thought you had some more time?"

I peered inside. Takeaway menus, the light bill and some other nonsense that would wait a bit longer. "He felt it necessary to impress upon me the importance of his deadline."

"You OK? Any ringing in the ears? Nausea? Dizziness?"

I shook my head. "I know what a concussion is, Ash. The guy was looking to hurt me, but not enough to send me to emergency. I'm fine."

She took the mail from me. "C'mon, let's get upstairs. I'll take a look at that cut."

I fell into step behind her with a short laugh.

"What?" she grunted at me over her shoulder.

"Nothing," I said. "I didn't realize you cared, is all."

As we got to the door she was, as always, unfazed by my attempts at banter. "I care about lots of things," she said. "Like getting paid."

"All I deal with these days are mercenaries."

"When this over, you can make new friends," she said, cocking her head to my name on the pebbled glass. "Open up, pretty boy."

Any ice left in that tray would be a godsend. I gripped the handle as I fished the keys loose, and the door swung open.

We exchanged glances.

"You forget to lock up?"

I shook my head.

Ayesha unzipped her bomber jacket. I could see, once again, the heavy swell on her hip peeking out from under her hoodie, forged dark steel and semi-automatic peace of mind.

"Hello?" I called out. No answer, but I could hear music, fuzzy and distant. As I got closer, I realized it was from headphones, something British and oh-so-indie.

I stepped in. The track suit bottoms had been traded in for skinny Verdigo designer jeans, the Chuck Taylors swapped for pointed toe pumps. But I recognized the easy posture leaning those legs on the front desk very quickly, the relaxed tilt of her head.

I never asked for the key back.

I took the seat in front of her, waiting for her to notice.

She lowered her feet, looking up from the laptop's screen. Its blue light flattered her face, her smile widening bit as she took me in. She tugged the white buds loose from her ears.

"Hi Thad," she said. She lowered the laptop's lid, sealing it with a gentle click.

"Hi," I said. "Good to see you, Charlie."

Neither of us said anything. I could hear car horns bleating outside, the buzz coming from her removed headphones, my pulse starting to pick up a bit of steam, a steady rhythm.

"You too." She was nice enough to at least appear sincere. In front of her she had what looked like a takeaway cup of white tea. She sipped it purposefully, holding my gaze for a moment. She dipped her head towards the laptop and the seemingly ceaseless pile of paperwork on my desk.

"So," she said. "How's business?"

"You should really turn that down," I said, nodding to her headphones. "That kind of volume is putting you in Pete Townshend territory."

"I think I'll be fine."

I heard the tugging of a zipper behind me, Ayesha closing her jacket, apparently satisfied with the threat level. She stepped from behind me.

"Hey," she said to the young woman at the desk.

"Hey," Charlie responded. "All right?"

Ayesha shot me an *Everything OK?* look. I shrugged.

"Who's this?" Ayesha asked.

Charlie looked at me with a slight smile, apparently equally anxious for the answer.

"Ayesha Gill, this is Charlotte Colbourne," was all I said.

Charlie's smile went a little sad then, a dip at the corner of her mouth.

I took off my jacket and unbuttoned my shirt, heading to the small kitchenette. I opened the freezer and pulled loose the ice tray. A few remained, thank God. I dumped the cubes onto a paper towel and pressed them to my cheek. I sat on the couch, trying not to wince.

They were both looking at me, clearly expecting something more.

I slowly lowered myself onto the cushions.

"She used to work here," I said, shrugging again.

30

"You want to tell me about the case?" Charlie asked. We had moved to my office, where I rummaged at my desk and she sat across. I had sent Ayesha out to get some lunch.

"Can't," I said.

"I'm still covered by my confidentiality paperwork."

I opened my own laptop. As it hummed to life, I looked over the screen at her, sitting where she had sat many times before, sitting with the same questions about cases, the same eager smile.

"You don't work here," I said. "It's just a bit weird now, y'know?"

She sat back, crossed her arms, and uncrossed them just as quickly.

"Sure," she said. "Sure, I get it."

"What are you doing here?" I asked, careful to keep my voice neutral.

"Saw something about the case in the papers," she said. "I know a couple of folks over at Bergman Hapsburg, and one of them mentioned there was a PI involved, fellow with a funny name."

I smiled a little.

"So, not my hardest case," she said.

"How's the new job?" I asked. "Still liking it?"

"It's good. But it's been six months now. Not really new any more."

"Six months?"

She nodded.

"Wow. Well, time flies when you're having fun, right?"

She looked at the mess of my desk, the horror show of manila envelopes, yellow notepads and empty coffee cups.

"Yeah. Looks like a right blast," she said.

We sat quietly for a bit. She tilted her head, giving a spot under her jawline a quick scratch.

"Anyhow," she said. "Thought I might be able to help a bit. I still have my license, you know."

"Probationary license," I replied. "But yes, I know you do."

"Didn't realize you had brought someone else on board," she said.

"Ayesha's a freelancer, and she's not really the office type," I said. "I'm doing OK in here by myself, but I still need eyes and ears out there."

She picked up an envelope from the pile, turning it to face me. There was something seemingly angry and red in block letters on it. I shrugged.

"OK, I'm behind. Look, it's busy here. Work has been steady for months now."

"So get a temp in."

"Sure. Got your old agency's number?" Charlie had started here as an office temp before graduating to investigator last year.

She opened her purse.

"Might do, actually. Unless you were just being a bastard, of course."

She looked up from the open bag.

"There may have been a whiff of bastardness around that comment," I acknowledged.

She snapped the purse shut.

"Do whatever you want, but don't talk down to me. I know you're angry I left."

"You can do whatever you want," I countered. "I'm fine."

"It was a good offer. And it was in my field."

"Is that what Royce had to say?" I said. Her boyfriend— they had been serious for about eight months or so. "You didn't even finish grad school, Chuck."

She smiled then, but not the kind she had shown before, the kind that wanted validation. This was more in tune with the smiles I had seen from a lot of women—somewhere between bemusement and disappointment.

"I make my own decisions, but yes—he did suggest that

134

perhaps working at an NGO promoting economic development might be better for me then running around in the middle of the night taking pictures of people faking insurance injuries."

"To be fair, we also do a lot of background checks and security consulting here," I said. "And I'm guessing not a lot of the girls you work with at that NGO have shoes quite as nice."

Ayesha stepped into the main office, interrupting Charlie's response. She swept in with a paper bag full of sandwiches and a tray of coffees. She distributed them quickly and without comment, finally plopping into the chair next to Charlie, who simply sipped her coffee, looking straight ahead.

"Thanks," I said, unwrapping my club.

"No worries," she said. She dumped some cream into her own coffee, stirring quickly and bringing it to her mouth. No one had said anything else since she arrived, and Charlie had made no motion towards her own food.

"Not hungry?" Ayesha asked.

Charlie shook her head, a quick twitch.

"Hunh," Ayesha said, taking another sip form her coffee and switching her gaze from Charlie to me. "Weird energy in here, yeah?"

31

When my phone buzzed shortly after lunch, I was more than happy to step out to take the call, even if it was Shane Bowering on the other end. I made it way outside to the street below. Bit of fresh air might help, I reasoned.

"Grayle," he said by way of greeting. "Where's my book report?"

Shit. "I'll have it sent over in a bit, but I'll save you the read. Your kid is clean."

"Yeah?"

"Oh yeah. Squeaky. He knows some rough types but, by all accounts and observations, he is a bit of a Boy Scout. He's solid."

"Hunh," Bowering mused.

"What? I thought that would be good news."

"Well, I mean it's great he's an upstanding member of society and all, but now I am in a position of knowing my offer of further work could corrupt him."

"Then don't. You said yourself he's a good enough bartender. Keep him there."

"Damn it all," Bowering moaned. "Hard to find good help these days, in some areas at least."

"Maybe have a job fair. An outreach program to local schools."

"You're pretty funny for a guy who almost forgot to deliver his promised work to me," Bowering observed.

"Well, that's fair. But I got a bit going on right now."

"Yeah? How's that?"

I pulled the phone away from my face, turning my face towards the unseasonably warm February sun.

"You there?" he asked.

"Yeah. I'm here."

136

"Let's have it."

I sighed.

"I'm into Quigley."

Now it was my turn to wait as Bowering presumably needed a moment to collect his wits, and if not those, certainly a bit of outrage.

"Grayle," he said after a second. "You stupid, stupid man."

"Would it matter if I told you it was for a good reason and borne of the very best of intentions?"

"Do good intentions power wheelchairs? Because that's what you're facing if you don't square this."

"I know."

"*Do* ya, though?" he almost yelled. "Cripes, this could be bad news all around."

"Calm down," I said. "What do you care, anyways?"

Another pause. I could hear Bowering sucking air through his teeth.

"Quigley outsources on occasion. I'm one of his go-to guys to connect him with muscle."

I laughed. "I think we're clear. I already had a visit form whoever is going to be bashing skulls in a few days. And you're no pasty Irishman with a bad haircut."

"Grayle," Bowering said. "I took the sheet. Tall guy, dark hair, flat on Seven Sisters Road?"

"You know where I live?"

"And where you work," he said, rattling off the address.

"Why'd you take this? And why doesn't it have my name?"

"I took it because this is my job, or at least part of it. And we don't usually use names. Description, addresses, routines, sure. Photos when the day comes. Not knowing the ID gives us at least some, whattya call it—deniability."

"If you get pinched, you mean."

"Well, my guys. I don't do that stuff myself anymore. And they don't get pinched for this stuff, ever."

"How long did he give you?"

"Few days," Bowering said. "He was straight with you on that much, at least."

"Don't suppose you could send the bartender to do it. Like

137

you said, he seems a gentle soul."

Bowering's laugh was short, and to the point.

"Yeah, that's not an option. Look, just get the money, and this all goes away," he said.

My phone twitched, and I stole a quick glance at it. A text from Ayesha: LET'S GO.

"Working on it," I said. "Might have a break on the case."

"Here's hoping."

Following my few dealings with him, I felt it safe to safe to say Shane Bowering was not a man given to introspection. He was, in his criminally specific niche market, a ruthless capitalist—a pursuit that left little wriggle room for things like empathy.

Still, I decided to push my luck. Desperation has a way of making one oddly optimistic.

"I'm in for ten grand," I said.

"Well, that's not great, but it's not exactly the end of the world. Can you get it from someone else?"

Here goes. "I thought you could spot me it."

Bowering laughed again, a chuckle cut through with pure pity. "I'm going to assume that was more of your famous wit."

"C'mon. I'm scrambling here, and like I said: I got a good shot at covering this very soon."

"No chance. I'm sorry, but you have proven yourself to be a risk."

"Jesus, I'm not asking for a small business loan or something."

"You'd have better luck," he said. "because in our market, you are a proven credit risk. You're on the hook to a psychopathic Irish gangster and loan shark. So, this is a no go. I won't cover you."

"Hey, I'd rather be into you than Quigley."

I heard the snap of a Zippo case on the other end, and a deep, slow drag.

"No, son," Bowering said, letting loose a stream of smoke on the other end. "You really don't."

32

Following Ayesha's next and even less patient text, I found her around the corner waiting, drumming her fingers on the dashboard of a sleek, pearl-grey Mercedes. The speakers in back were shaking as music pounded the interior. She was in the passenger seat.

Charlie was in the driver's.

"Get in," Ayesha said, lowering her window.

I tapped on the driver side glass.

"Yes?" Charlie sweetly asked.

"I'm sorry, but I think Ayesha and I can find our own way."

"She offered to drive," Ayesha shouted over the music.

"Can you turn that down?" I asked.

"C'mon Thad," Ayesha called out over the booming hip-hop, not hearing what I said—or possibly ignoring it. "Get in."

I lowered myself close to Charlie's face.

"Why are you doing this?"

"We talked about the case," she said. "When you went outside to talk to your loan shark."

"He's *a* loan shark, not mine. And how the hell do you know about that?"

Charlie dipped her head towards Ayesha, who was now lost in the chorus.

"For Christ's sake," I muttered. "Did she even pretend to hold out a little?"

"Nah," Charlie said. "She wanted to know what it was like working with you when I was there, so we swapped a couple of stories. She made a call about where this Copta guy is right now, and I said I'd give you a lift."

"And hold onto this," Ayesha said, holding up the satchel with Duclos recent financial activity. She tossed it into the back.

"Yeah, that too," Charlie said. Then, to me: "She's kind of a bad ass, hunh?"

I closed my eyes, hoping this would all be much different when I reopened them. No such luck.

I leaned towards the driver's window

"Why are you doing this?" I asked again.

Charlie gripped and un-gripped the steering wheel, spreading her fingers wide, and I could see the perfect nails, painted hot-rod red and as sleek and unblemished as this Merc's paintjob.

"It's just a ride," she said. "Don't be so dramatic."

I grabbed the back door, driver's side.

"Where to?" I asked.

"Where do ya think?" Ayesha said. "Guy's on his yacht. You had that thing, would you spend a lot of time elsewhere?"

"Probably not. Of course, I'd settle for his car. Spare me a lot of worries about every last bump and groan my Saab makes."

Charlie dropped the car into gear, and it purred to action, gliding onto Morwell before doubling back to Oxford Street.

"We got a good deal on the lease," she said. "Besides, Ayesha said business was good. You could always treat yourself for once."

"That money has been spoken for, but thanks," I replied. It was, of course, slow going in the heart of downtown London. "What else did you tell here?" I called out to Ayesha, who mercifully, finally turned the music down a bit.

"Pretty much all of it," Ayesha said. "What's the big deal? She worked cases with you before."

"Yeah, Thad," Charlie said, meeting my eyes in the rear-view mirror. "What's the big deal?"

I was determined not to be seen sulking, so I simply shrugged. "No big deal. Let's get to Copta and see what he knows about all this."

"So you think he killed the mum?" Charlie asked.

"Maybe, yeah," I mused. I poked Ayesha's shoulder. "You really didn't spare a single detail, did you?"

She smiled. "Relax—this might all be over very soon."

"Yeah, we reckon Copta might've done the mom," I continued. "But we're not sure why. We are pretty sure they were having an affair, though, so it makes sense Copta killed Duclos."

"Maybe Copta kills the other because he did all that and she wants to break it off?" Charlie mused.

"Yeah. And what about the kid?" Ayesha said. "Why leave him alive if he knew about the affair?"

"The kid?"

"Yeah, sorry. The Duclos have a boy. Around 12."

"Wow," Charlie said, again meeting my eyes in the rearview. "What's the son like?"

"Quiet. Book nerd. Awkward. Thad likes him."

"You don't say," Charlie replied, trying to find my eyes. I had turned away. "Maybe he didn't know what was going on," she added.

"He knew," I said.

"He's convinced the son had some idea about the affair," Ayesha said. "I don't think it matters."

"So why not go to the cops?" Charlie asked.

Ayesha and I were quiet for a moment.

"Guys," Charlie said. "C'mon."

"Your old boss took this on contingency," Ayesha said. "There's a lot of money missing, so if we can find it before the cops—"

"Jesus, Thad." Charlie somehow managed to sound exasperated and disappointed in equal measure.

The sun had climbed a bit, and despite the window's tint, I slid on my shades.

"It's my neck," I said. "No one else's."

"It's not all his fault," Ayesha said.

"Thanks, but I don't need you to explain on my behalf," I said.

"She already told me about Brock pulling a runner," Charlie said, matching my tone and velocity. "I still can't believe he hung you out like that."

"They went back a bit, right?" Ayesha said.

Charlie nodded. "Yeah. They were friends for, like, ever."

I watched the streets pass, the crush of people happily carrying on with their days, an almost even mix of briefcases and shopping bags dotting the sidewalks. I stretched out, making use of the leg room.

"Yeah, well. what can I say?" I said. This time it was Charlie's eyes not to be seen in the mirror. "People have a way of letting you down sometimes."

33

At the wharf. Ayesha and I hopped out. Charlie cut the engine and made to open her door. I stepped in front of it.

"What?" she asked.

"Stay here," I said. She rolled her eyes.

"I still have my license. And I drove you guys here. C'mon, you're being silly."

I didn't move out of the way, but lowered my head a bit closer to her window.

"Look," I said, my voice a bit low. "I have no idea how this is going to go. But we need to talk to this guy because we still haven't found the guy we really need."

"Yeah, so? I know the basics, Thad."

"This isn't some small-timer or a guy faking a back injury. Besides, what time did you tell what's-his-name you'd be home?"

Charlie smiled then, a thin little slit across her mouth.

"You know what his name is," she said.

"Royce," I said.

"Yes. Royce," she said.

I looked across the top of the car. Ayesha was adjusting that peace-of-mind lump on her hip, re-holstering it after checking the clip. I was happy that Charlie was looking at me than at her. Satisfied it was concealed, Ayesha shot me an impatient look. Time to go.

"We also might need to get out of here in a hurry," I said, standing and—I hoped—ending the argument. "Keep it running."

Charlie shrugged, and tilted the seat back a bit. Satisfied, Ayesha and I strode towards the St. Katherine's docks.

"What was that about?" she asked.

"Nothing. Told her to wait, is all."

I picked up the pace. Ayesha easily kept up.

"How'd you find out Copta's whereabouts?" I asked her.

"I had drinks with one of the guys from the party on his yacht. He said he's having some folks in today."

"Seriously?" I asked, amused. "One of those City boys?'

She smiled. "What can I say? Rich and dumb is kind of my wheelhouse."

Copta's yacht was open and bustling. We could hear loud laughs ringing out before we even got close to the stern. We stopped.

"What's the plan?" she asked.

"We get him alone and tell him we know about the affair. See if we can jolt him into yakking about anything else. He's got to know something."

"You still don't like him for clipping the husband?"

I shook my head. We were almost to the boat.

"No. But you kill the woman you're having an affair with whose husband is missing, a good reason to do it might be if she knew where he was—or was going to get him back."

No sign of Copta as we approached the deck, however. Instead, a bloated, poplin-shirted guest was up and about, regaling the gathered with boasts of both his alleged economic and sexual prowess, pausing only to pick shrimp from his plate. Circled around him was a collection of about half-a-dozen of the rich and imperious, called in for what looked to be a pretty impressive brunch date. The usual high-end wares were being made available: Salmon terrine, eggs Benedict, bagels and lox. Plus, based on the volume and general energy coming off the boat, the Caesars and mimosas had been flowing and well-refreshed.

"Morning," I called out from the dock.

The fat man turned and saw me. If he was annoyed or worried, he didn't show it.

"Hello, hello," he called out, jovially. "To what do we owe the pleasure? Never mind, come aboard. Room for plenty. Welcome."

Not the reception I had expected, considering how we had left this boat the last time. I shot Ayesha a quick glance—*Is this guy for real?*—and she replied by stepping off the dock and onto the back of the yacht. I followed her lead. She picked up a flute of champagne.

"What brings you by?" he asked, reclining. "Looking for someone?"

"We were hoping to have a word with Mr. Copta," I said. A young woman in catering whites offered me quiche from a tray. I shook my head.

"Mr. Copta is otherwise detained. My name is Baxter. He and I work together."

I coughed politely. Ayesha took a respectable swig from her glass.

"Well, this is business. There is new information that needs to be discussed," I said, straining over the chatter of the guests around me.

Baxter cupped his hand by his ear, smiling apologetically—and broadly. He was enjoying himself.

I was not.

"Baxter," I said, raising my voice. "It's either we talk to your boss here or he can talk to Scotland Yard later this afternoon—say, around four o'clock?"

The chatter slowed considerably. I heard one of the guests —another huge man, this one with a splotch of hollandaise on his shirt—clear his throat, its waddle vibrating accordingly. The beautiful young woman linked to his left arm dabbed the front stain to keep busy and have somewhere to put her eyes. The scraping of cutlery faded away.

Magnus, the driver, emerged. He had a plate, one he quickly lay down as he stepped towards us. Out of the corner of my eye, I saw Ayesha make a half-step closer to me, on my right.

He dabbed the corner of his mouth with a cloth napkin, brilliantly white and clean.

"Thank you Baxter. I'll take this from here. Mr. Grayle, Mr. Copta is booked up for four o'clock," he said. "So maybe we should talk now."

I nodded in agreement. He waved us to follow, and led us to Copta's bedroom, where he and I had first spoken.

"Some bash," I said.

145

"It's been like that for the last couple of days."

"Why's your boss missing the party?" I asked.

Magnus ignored the question as we got to the door, closed. He knocked. No answer. He opened the door and strode in.

Copta's room was as we had left it, a testament to opulence as well as functionality. He again sat at the end of the bed, Magnus blocking the door. I stood in front of Copta, Ayesha just behind me, her stance bladed so she kept an eye on the way out.

"So," Copta said, taking a healthy pull from his own champagne glass. "What brings you by yet again?"

"I think you should speak to them, Mr. Copta," Magnus said. "Could be serious."

Copta smiled.

"Is that so. Well, Mr. Grayle, what is this new information that brought you here to embarrass me in front of my friends and crash my soiree?" He emptied the glass and stood, heading to the bar on the other side of the room.

"You heard about Annie Duclos?" I asked.

Copta nodded. He decided against more champers and instead poured a heavy splash of scotch over a single ice cube.

"Yes. I did," he said. His voice was thick.

I cast a quick look at his man at the door.

"You really want to do this with the hired help here?" I asked.

"Fuck you," Magnus snarled.

Copta shrugged.

"Shut up," Ayesha snapped at Magnus. "Thad, c'mon. Let's get on with it."

Copta had sat again. I sat next to him. He looked at me, puzzled and amused. I crossed my hands in my lap and leaned forward a bit. He matched my posture.

"We're pretty sure you were sleeping with Annie," I said.

He shrugged again.

"C'mon," I said. "No reason to hide behind propriety now."

He took another deep gulp from the heavy tumbler in his hand—crystal, by the look of it. A nice one. I watched Ayesha out of the corner of my eye. She wasn't stupid or brazen

146

enough to put her hand on her hip here, but I could see it hovering close enough by she could get to what was there fast enough. Magnus was apparently over my slight—his face was impassive, unmoved. He had either heard this before or didn't care.

Copta let out a stream of air through his lips, steady and long.

"I suppose Vivian isn't too common a name," he finally allowed.

So far, so good.

He began to rise, seeking a top-up. I reached out and touched his shoulder.

"Need you sober, or close to it," I said.

Copta acquiesced, sitting back down. Magnus shifted. He knew his boss wasn't anywhere near straight.

"Thad," Ayesha said, her voice tundra-cold. "Jesus, get a move on."

I ignored her. "How long were you guys together?" I asked him.

"About a year and a half, all told," Copta replied. His eyes were glassy, and I couldn't tell if it was the booze or something else, welling up from inside.

"How'd it start?"

"How do these things ever start?" he said. "We saw each other at a couple of functions, I made up a reason to get her number, we spent some time together." He sighed. "Her husband did a lot of work for me. It wasn't… that hard."

"You got an alibi? Gonna hold up when we talk to the cops?"

He nodded.

"How about your boy?" I asked, nodding towards Magnus. If he heard me, he didn't let it show.

Copta nodded again.

"I didn't do it," our host said. A new layer of glass glazed his eyes.

"I had a feeling," I said. I took the empty glass from his hand and laid it on the corner of the bed.

"Do you know who did?" Ayesha said, her voice sharp.

147

Copta looked up at her.

"No," he said, his voice finally steady. "No, I don't."

"And if he did, I imagine that would already have been addressed," I said.

I rose, standing over Copta.

"Do you know where Duclos is?" I asked. "Or the money?"

Copta shook his head.

"Think hard on this," I said. "'Cause he's still missing, and if he's alive he needs to know what's going on. And if he's dead—"

"I didn't kill him—"

I held up my hand.

"We know about the gambling. We know about that—" I nodded towards the stack of mail, the one with the crown, on his desk "—so what's your connection?"

Copta looked at the cards and shook his head.

"They invited me to play. I'm rich, Grayle. You should see the stuff people ask me to attend, spend money on, play with. It's all part of the deal."

"Did you get Duclos into that game, get him in trouble with these lunatics?"

"No," he said, his voice rising for the first time. "I did not."

"Why'd you help the cops?" Ayesha asked. "Didn't it work out great for you, Duclos being out of the picture while you were sitting pretty with the missus?"

Copta made to lie down. I gently pulled him back up to a sitting position.

"Annie asked me to help them," he said. "She needed him back. Said a son needs his father. I think she still loved him, to be honest. I mean, she loved me, but what do I know." He blinked. Tears were close. "A marriage is a complicated thing, I suppose. She missed him."

And that four million, I thought.

"Copta, listen to me: We gotta find him. That's it. There's still a lot here that needs answering, and a lot that needs cleaning up. If you know anything, and I mean *anything,* now would be a good time to come clean."

"Hang on," Magnus said, rousing from his dispassionate

sentry duties. "Why are you lot here and not the cops?"

"I'm under a bit of a deadline here," I said. "So I need any info you have as fast as possible."

"I told you before," Copta said. "I'm out of the game. I was helping the cops, for God's sake."

"You gotta know something or somebody," Ayesha said.

"Why are we even talking to these two?" Magnus said, his voice rising. "Mr. Copta, let's go—"

Copta stood and faced me. Magnus shut up.

"I don't know anything else that could help," he said. "I would if I could."

'That alibi better hold up," I said. "The cops will be here. Count on it."

"I'm not worried," he said. He nodded to Magnus and headed back to the bar.

"Let's go," Magnus said.

"Hang on," Ayesha said. "Thad—"

"Yeah. Let's go," I said.

She stared at me, amazed. The only sound in the room was the ice hitting the bottom of Copta's well-used glass.

"Jesus, we don't have *anything*," she snapped after a moment. "You're just going to walk out of here?"

I took in the room: the art, the bed, the lush rug, the bar. Copta had yet to turn around, lost in thought, in his mourning. Underneath my feet, I could feel the slightest roll of the water underneath this yacht, this bloated cathedral. Copta turned to wobble back to his bed, his face red and puffy.

"And some people have everything," I said. "And look how goddamned happy they are. Let's go."

34

Back in the Mercedes. Ayesha was still brooding. We drove in silence for a while. I knew Charlie well enough to know she may have correctly read the mood, but it was only a matter of time before her curiosity got the better of her and she asked how it all shook out. I struck pre-emptively.

"He didn't do it, Ayesha," I said. "Look at him. He's a mess."

"Sure, or maybe he's just a falling down drunk."

"Literally nothing we have seen so far supports that," I said. "Face it. He loved her. He didn't kill her. And he sure as hell doesn't know where Duclos is."

Stony silence settled upon us again. Charlie turned on the radio.

"We're fucked," Ayesha said.

"What do you want me to do?" I demanded. "I can't make the guy admit to killing her when he, you know, *didn't.*"

"So, uh, you guys hungry…?" Charlie said, sliding onto Shoreditch High Street. "'Cause it looks like we've got a day ahead."

"We'll send out when we get back to the office," I said. I turned back to Ayesha. "Why are you so pissed, anyways? We can tell Dunsmore the *Vivian* tip, they'll interview him—if he's lying, they'll find out, and even if he's not, we get a few brownie points for helping the investigation."

"Until she asks why you went by yourselves first," Charlie piped in.

"Yeah, thanks," I said. "But we still figured it out first."

"Don't think they'll be patting us on the back too hard for that," Ayesha said.

"Hey, I'm just trying to stay optimistic here."

Ayesha turned in her seat and faced me.

"You're broke. In a few days a crew of Irish madmen are going to grab you and work you over, big time. Then a few days after that they're going to do it again. And then they'll say you now owe them more money. Plus, I guarantee you that whatever happens, Dunsmore is going to make your life scorched earth hell, especially if she doesn't get that promotion. She'll do everything she can to get your license, and she will, because you're a mess of a human being who thinks being clever is the same as being smart. You'll be lucky to get a job as a Waitrose security guard."

"Interesting you led with the me-being-broke part," I said. "Worried about getting paid?"

"Oh, for—" she started, her teeth flashing, before Charlie jumped in.

"Enough," she said, loudly and firmly. "Everyone relax. Thad, how much are you in for?"

"Oh no," I said. "Forget it."

Charlie looked pointedly at Ayesha.

"Don't—" I said.

"He needs about ten grand," she said. "And more soon. That's how this works."

"I have money," Charlie said.

I sighed.

"Royce has money, but thank you," I said. "And I can still figure this out."

"You're running out of time," Charlie said.

"If we can find Duclos, we have a good chance," I said.

"Forget it," Ayesha said. "He's dead. If he was alive, he'd have come out of hiding by now. His wife got murdered, for God's sake."

"Yeah, but didn't you say he might have had some mental health issues, based on who you talked to?" Charlie said. "The murder might have really messed him up, driven him deeper underground."

I rubbed my temples, hard, trying to coax some more blood flow through my weary skull.

"Both those are possible. Probable, even. But that doesn't mean there's not an angle we're missing," I said. I picked up

151

the file again, and felt my insides sag a little with how heavy it was in my hand. "Did you get to check this out?" I asked Charlie.

"You guys weren't gone that long, but I gave it a quick look," she said. I smiled, in spite of myself. I knew it—of course she couldn't resist. I would've been disappointed otherwise.

"And? Anything?" Ayesha said.

Charlie shook her head.

"It's just the last year or so," she said. "Pretty standard stuff. Bills, mostly: Cable, Internet, the mortgage, some home reno stuff, plus a few small-time investments here and there. Just enough to keep everything looking totally legit, I guess." We were at a red light—she leaned her elbow against the door and rested her cheek in her hand. "There's no Post-It that says, 'My secret Swiss accounts can be found here', if that's what you were wondering."

"I'm embarrassed to admit how much I was hoping for that," I said, leaning back and flipping open the folder. "But be that as it may—this is all we got now."

Traffic was slow. I felt anxious, caged even, in this barely-moving Mercedes.

"So, what's your angle?" Ayesha asked.

"How's that?" I said.

"You said we were missing an angle, something we hadn't considered. What is it?"

I sat up, taking in the stream of pedestrians. The car finally lurched ahead.

"I dunno," I admitted. "Except maybe if he's alive, the only thing that makes sense is he doesn't know what's going on."

Charlie returned to playing with the radio. Ayesha clicked her teeth against her thumbnail. I picked up the folder and began leafing through it. Unsurprisingly for Duclos, everything was neatly ordered, money going out every month for the day-to-day of adult life, one after the other, rows upon rows of tiny stagnant numbers boxed into their spreadsheet homes:

Cable
Internet
Mortgage
Phone(s)
Tuition
Home renovation
Insurance (car/home/life/other)
Entertainment (includes magazines and restaurants)
Gas
Car Payment

Normally, I'd be quick to dismiss something this achingly organized and face-meltingly mundane, but as most of my monthly paperwork is in a shoe box on my kitchen table, I've lost the high ground, to be sure. I flipped through more.

Insurance (car/home/life/other)

"Hey, what insurance do you guys have?" I asked.

"I dunno," Charlie said. "Standard stuff. This car is covered, uh… our flat, I'm sure?"

"I have life insurance," Ayesha said. "Seemed an ironic purchase after I left the military, but here we are."

I flipped through, tracing the bills to the beginning of last year.

There was a cheque made out to Sirius Insurance. New policy. Extra insurance on the Duclos' house to cover what seemed to be extensive renovations.

Yet Annie Duclos had complained about the house need a big facelift and nothing had been done with it for years.

Hunh.

I double-checked the payment and pulled out my notes. Cheque was cut early last year, soon as the work was done— all around a time when Annie had been away.

I dug around my pockets, finally finding the card.

Elmore Cranston. The old friend from school, the guy who had Duclos help sell all those candy bars for his kid's volleyball team. In addition to apparently being a good father, he was also a Customer Service Specialist with Sirius Insurance.

"Hey," I said. I handed Charlie the card. "Pop that in the GPS. Let's go."

She peered at it.

"That's near Canary Wharf. In this traffic, we'll be there by Tuesday."

I grabbed the folder and hopped out.

"Hey!" Ayesha said.

"Get to the office, please—both of you," I said, cutting through the motionless cars. Someone honked once, weakly. "I'm taking the Tube to get to this guy's office," I shouted over my shoulder. "I'll check in as soon as I have anything."

Their faces said it all. Both frustrated, yet resigned. The outraged horns on the street began to bleat louder, each vying for its own attention, drowning out any protests that they may have been shouting my way.

35

Cranston's office turned out to be a disappointingly shabby cubicle. Despite the post code, his company maintained modest accommodations just outside the radius of the financial giants ensconced in this part of town. He was surprised to see me as I peered over the carpeted three-quarter wall a bored receptionist had pointed me towards, but despite how we had left our previous conversation, he was gracious enough to offer me a coffee from the ground floor newsagents.

"So what brings you by?" he asked, handing me a takeaway cup and taking a quick flip through the papers.

"I wanted to apologize," I said. "In my job, you see a lot of people's worst, and I think I might've been a bit quick to say some of the things I said."

"Not at all," he said, smiling genuinely. "Apology accepted." Sealing the deal, he tapped his cup against mine.

"Well, that's a relief," I said. "Thank you. But I have a couple more questions, if that's OK."

"I imagine you might. Terrible news about Annie."

"Yeah, it's a mess. But this is about Yannick."

Cranston took a sip.

"I don't think I know anything more than what I said before," he replied.

I held up the folder.

"Yannick took out a pile of extra insurance from you last year. Major construction job, apparently. Major construction that his wife definitely didn't know about. You know anything about that?"

Cranston buttoned the top of his suit jacket and straightened his already-straight tie. "Unless you're interested in talking about buying some insurance, Mr. Grayle, I am getting back to work. I don't have to talk to you or anyone else about my clients or their purchases." He turned back to his office building.

"Don't be dense," I said, grabbing his elbow. "This is a homicide investigation now. The only reason I'm here before the cops is they just haven't gotten to your name yet on the list of people I gave them."

"What 'list'?"

"The people I've interviewed about this case," I said. "That's what I gave the cops—the people who had a chance to tell everything they knew."

He froze.

"Cranston, c'mon," I said. "How do you think it's going to look when the cops knock on your door to ask you the same questions, and I have to tell them you knew something and didn't spill first chance you got?"

"I don't know anything for certain," he said.

"Well, I'll settle for what you might know."

He glanced around. Someone, likely a co-worker, walked by and nodded hello. "Can we go back upstairs?" he asked.

"I'm enjoying the sunshine," I said. "Let's go. Might as well get it over with."

He sighed, and I could almost see the last of any defiance draining from his chest. He pulled out his phone and, after some rapid thumbwork, I felt the soft rumble of my own mobile in my pocket. I pulled it loose and opened his e-mail, an exchange between he and Yannick about a year and a half ago.

My eyes widened.

"Are you serious?" I asked.

He nodded.

"Jesus... How long did this take?"

"Not long at all," he said, crossing his arms. "They put a tent around the place, made it look like an extermination. Anyone asked, they would've said a pipe burst. They were in and out in something like a week."

"Why didn't you tell me?"

"Why would I?" he said, standing a bit taller. "He's my friend. I was happy to help him."

I thought back to our first conversation, that little bit of venom that leaked from Cranston's mouth when Annie came up.

"You knew about the affair," I said. "You're covering for your guy."

He shrugged.

I scrolled through the e-mail, the full exchange about this deal between Cranston and Duclos from about a year and a half ago. I finally got to the part I was looking for.

"Help him, yeah—you did that, for sure," I said. "Plus, I'm guessing this whole thing was not exactly totally on the up-and-up. That's a big number, so I'm going to take a shot and say Yannick overpaid. Either for your silence or, hell, just because you guys go back a ways."

Cranston kept his nerve. "Just business," he said, forcing a smile.

I put my phone away.

"Well, either way, a nice payday for you. Still, though. Pretty impressive getting that all done so fast. I mean, a *week?*"

"When you're rich, you can get just about anything done," Cranston said, regaining a bit more of his composure, the weight finally off what passed for his conscience. "Timelines are for little people."

36

About an hour later. I sat in my Saab outside the Duclos' house in West Brampton, where this all began. I had plugged in my battered iPod and was listening to some music, blasting it really, while considering my next step here, the wisdom of this move. The phone buzzed.

"Hey," I said, killing the volume on The Clash. "How's things back at the ranch?"

"We're good, thanks. Got your message. Charlie sent out for pizza and we are getting all the paperwork and evidence together."

"Yeah, she's good like that."

"Well, she remembered your credit card info, so I think this one is on you."

I smiled. "Yeah, she's good like that, too."

"You ready to go?"

I rubbed my hands together, more nervous energy than the cold.

"Yeah, I think so," I said. "I don't think there's any danger. Assuming this is actually what happened. It's, uh, pretty crazy."

She laughed, a tight little chuckle from the back of her throat. Ayesha had a lovely laugh. I would have to remember to tell her that sometime, when everything got back to normal.

"You gotta admit, it makes a lot of sense," she said.

"Well it beats the current working theory, which is non-existent."

"Didn't you say something about lack of options streamlining the decision-making process?" she asked.

"Once or twice," I said. I killed the car and buttoned my coat.

"Heading in?" she asked.

"Yep."

"OK. I can meet you there, you know."

"Nah. This should be over in a few," I said, stepping out into the street and jogging across the road. "I'll message if I get in trouble."

"Hang on," she said. She handed the phone off.

"Thad?" Charlie said.

"Hey."

The briefest of pauses.

"Be careful, OK?" she said.

I stopped in front of the Duclos house. Yellow police tape swathed the front door. No matter. That's not where I was headed.

"Yeah, of course," I said.

"OK. We'll save some pizza, but you'll need to get back in one piece to enjoy it."

"One slice of pepperoni will be enough. I'm keeping the winter weight at bay."

"Big Valentine's date coming up?"

"Oh, yeah, totally," I said, angling around the corner of the house and heading out back. "Did I tell you I got that Ingrid Bergman box set?"

"Shame to keep her waiting, then. See you soon." She hung up.

I hopped the fence separating the front of the Duclos house and driveway from the front and landed with a soft thud on the grass.

Across from me was the office shed Annie had pointed out when we first met.

The door was locked, but not in any way convincingly. Two hard drives of my heel below the latch and I was in. There was a small desk, a closed laptop, two shelves with books organized alphabetically by author and subject, and a single lamp. In other words, the office was everything Duclos I had seen was: Clean. Organized. Spartan.

Empty.

I rolled back the small oval rug in the middle of the floor, careful of the wire that connected it to the trapdoor beneath.

From there, I worked my fingers into the floorboards until I found the latch.

Success.

It opened, and I was face to face with another door. A hatch.

I punched in the code Cranston had provided. The lock clicked. I turned the wheel, opened it up, and took one last deep breath.

What was that line?

"Once more unto the breach, dear friends, once more."

Right. Or as someone else might say, *Here goes nothing.*

Leaving the hatch open, I carefully stepped onto the ladder and lowered myself into the darkness. I could hear a faint tapping, just loud enough to be made out over the sound of the blood pounding through my ears. As I got closer to the bottom, the light grew. I stepped off the ladder and turned.

It was a simple room, the tiniest of fortresses: a single cot, a cement wall shelved full of canned goods and a steel, prison-style toilet.

And there, with his back to me, typing furiously away on one of three giant screens in front of him and nodding along to whatever was playing on a pair of oversized headphones, sat Yannick Duclos.

I felt lightheaded with relief and thumbed a quick text to Ayesha. As I slid my phone away, he turned slightly to consult a binder, and caught me in the corner of a bleary eye.

"Hey," I said. I raised both my hands in a 'I mean no harm' gesture.

He slowly pulled the headphones off, gingerly laying them down.

"Who are you?" he asked.

I took two steps towards him. He stood, backing into his desk.

"Yannick, there is a lot we need to talk about. Some of it is going to be tough, and there are people who have a lot of questions for you. But you need to come with me."

"Who are you?" he repeated. "How'd you find me?"

"My name is Thaddeus Grayle. I'm a private detective. Your wife hired me to find you."

"My wife?" he snorted. "Of course. It took all this for her to notice I was even gone, I'm sure."

"Yeah," I said. "Look, you might want to sit down. There's a lot to cover."

"No, there's not," he said. "I need to get back to work."

I looked around the room, spartan and desolate.

"Are you... serious?" I asked. "We need to go, Yannick. This isn't a joke."

"Sure it is," he said, sitting down and going to back to his keyboard and screens. "I've got work to do. You can stare at the back of my head, maybe have some soup if you fancy it, or you can piss off. I'm not bothered."

He resumed typing.

I strode to the desk and jerked the chair towards me. "Listen to me. This isn't how I wanted this to play out, but you need to know. Your wife is dead. She was shot, in your house. The police are going to want to speak to you."

"I didn't do it," he said, calmly.

"Yeah, well, I don't see anyone here who can corroborate that alibi."

He nodded to a camera in the corner. "That will. I haven't been out of here in over a week."

"Jesus Christ," I nearly shouted. "Are you absorbing this information in any way? Are you *listening* to me?"

He regarded me, curiously.

"Yes, I am. I am, however, concerned you're not listening to me. I need to finish this work."

"What could possibly be so goddamned importan—"

He cut me off with a wave of his hand. Standing he pointed to the screens.

"If you found me here, it's safe to assume you know a lot of my life already, so I will cut to the chase. I can't leave. I'm working to pay off a debt. I'm here hiding because it is important to those I am working for that they can monitor me and keep me on their leash."

"Who are you working for?"

"The Albanians," he said. "They asked me to move some money for them. The margins were just too good to be true. I agreed. Then it all went south—perhaps inevitably."

I took in the screens, the scrolling numbers, the splayed binders and files.

"They told you the money you were working with was flagged?" I ventured. "Or you got busted through some banking software and they had to cut and run. All gone, and you had to work to make it back, right?"

He nodded. "How'd you guess?"

"An old scam. Drug dealers have been doing it forever. You get some patsy to move your product, you pay some other guys to rob him and bring the product back to you, then bam— you own him. He works for you, now and forever."

He nodded.

"They said I had to make it back. They threatened my family. They took all my money—"

My heart, pounding up to that point, began to freeze in my chest, my slowed blood feeling almost crystalline in my veins.

"What?" I managed.

"Oh yes. All gone," he said. "And I'm still on to clean about another—" he glanced down at his papers, "—8 million, I'd say. It was safer for me here, in the panic bunker. If I told Annie, she would've left me. Taken Aiden. I had already lost the money. I couldn't lose my son. Safer here. Safer to work. They said it wouldn't take much longer."

His voice hitched a bit.

"I wanted a place like this for some time," he said, voice low. "I used to go away sometimes, and now I had a place where I could go whenever I wanted."

I sat down, feeling my face go pale.

"What?" he asked.

"Nothing." I put my face in my hands, cradling my quickly-paling cheeks.

A painfully awkward pause ensued.

"Um," he said. "I'm sorry, but you're in my chair."

"Oh. Sorry." I stood and made my way over to the cot, regaining my composure a bit. He returned to his work.

"Yannick, look, we still gotta go. The cops want to talk to you. You gotta take care of your son now."

"I *am* taking care of my son," he snapped. "I'm trying to make sure we both survive this and we have a chance to start over somewhere."

"For shit's sake, there is no starting over here," I said. "Didn't you hear me? Forever, Yannick. You're in now to them forever. There is no reality where they let their little financial savant walk away from this."

I stood and strode towards him.

"You need to come with me. The cops can help protect you. You gotta get out in front of this."

I pushed my hand out, offering it to him.

"You have to trust me," I said.

"No," he said, glancing at the camera again. "For all I know this is a test of my loyalty."

"This is a test of your *intelligence*," I shouted. I reached out and grabbed his shoulders, roughly. "This is over. You're out of options. So come on—get up the fucking ladder."

He reached under his desk, pulling loose a pistol.

"I don't think so," he said. His eyes were darting around, and his speech was picking up speed. "No, no. We're staying here for as long as it takes. Until the work is done."

"Thad?"

I spun, hearing Ayesha's voice at the top of the hatch.

"Hey!" I cried back. "He's here. We're talking. Everything is going to be OK—right Yannick?"

He levelled the gun at me. I took as deep a breath as I could without it betraying my nerves.

"Everything is going to be OK because you're a smart guy," I said. "You know you're just panicking a bit right now. You're in some trouble, yeah, but it's fixable trouble."

Keeping the gun on me, he slid across the back wall and giving himself a clean line of sight and fire to the bottom of the ladder.

"You pulling that trigger, though, makes this a lot less fixable," I said.

He laughed, a short joyless bark.

"You said yourself, this isn't something I can walk away from," he said.

"Listen to me," I said. "Your son needs you to think this through. Just keep talking to me, stay with me here."

I caught Ayesha out of the corner of my eye, slowly coming into the light from the bottom of the ladder.

Duclos spun, training the gun on her.

Ayesha had hers out already, right hand on the grip and trigger, left hand underneath, holding it steady.

"Yannick," she said, her voice calm and smooth as a still lake. "Let's calm down."

He turned back to me.

"Any closer," he said, "And I will shoot him."

"Thad?" she asked. "You OK?"

"Yeah," I said. "Guess I should've asked you to come with."

She took some air in, sharply, between her closed teeth.

"Yeah. Well. I'm here now," she said.

She kept her gun on Yannick, her hands steady as a glacier.

"Yannick, all three of us are walking out of here," she said. "So I need you to stay calm and put the gun down. OK?"

Yannick still had his gun on me, but his hands were decidedly less steady than Ayesha's. It had drooped a bit, low enough that he would probably take my kneecap off if he squeezed the trigger.

She stepped forward.

"Stop," he said, his voice quavering. He raised the gun back to my eye line.

She took another step.

"STOP," he repeated.

"Yannick…" she said.

He looked back at his desk. The screens were still flickering at us from across the ways, the number scrolling.

I hadn't noticed it before, but taped to the edge of one of the monitors was a picture of Aiden, struggling to smile for the school photographer.

"I'm staying," he said, his voice calm. He turned the gun from me and pointed it now at Ayesha.

"Yannick," she said again. "There are lots of ways out of this."

He pulled the trigger.

I leapt across, unable to get to him before Ayesha returned fire. Duclos and I collapsed heavily on the floor. My ears were howling, a high-pitched whine cutting through them. I turned him over.

Blood was coming from his mouth and ears.

"Oh Jesus," I said. I pulled his shirt loose from his waist, and found the wound. Lower abdomen. I pulled off my suit jacket and pressed it into him, trying to get some pressure down while pulling my phone loose.

"Ash!" I cried as Duclos clawed at my arms and face. "Yannick, hang on, man. Hang on. *Ash!* Call 999!"

Yannick gurgled under me. I looked over my shoulder.

Ayesha was standing very still, but her right hand—her gun hand—had fallen to her side. She looked down at it quizzically for a moment, then slowly slid down the wall.

A smear of red on the white concrete followed her down.

"No no no no no *no*," came crashing out of my mouth. I rushed over to her side. She was reaching into her coat and shirt, trying to locate the entry wound.

I knelt beside her. Her breathing was ragged.

"Yannick," she said, her voice a low croak. "Help him."

"No," I said. I put my hand on hers, pressing in as hard as we could. I tried not to watch as her blood webbed around my fingers.

"The money," she said, her voice trailing off a bit.

"I don't care about the money," I said. "We gotta get you out of here."

"No," she whispered, her voice really laboring now. "Not. For you. The boy." She grabbed my wrist. "He needs to be taken care of," she whispered.

With her left hand, she showed me her phone.

"I'm calling," she murmured, her eyelids slipping. "Go."

I balled my fists, hard, for a half-second, then turned back to Duclos.

"Stay with me," I said to him. I resumed pressing onto the wound. He was pointing towards his desk

"You need something?" I asked. "What is it?" His eyes

were showing a lot of white. He jabbed his finger a bit harder.

"The picture? Is that it? You want Aiden's picture?" I started to kneel up but he grabbed me, shaking his head.

"Folder," he gasped. "Blue folder."

I bolted to the desk, and grabbed it. Blue folder, lots of tabbed pages, and on its front an embossed logo for Bergman Hapsburg—Duclos' employers. I fanned it open in front of him.

"What do you need?"

He reached up and grabbed it. His fingers smeared blood on the stark white paper. He flipped through to the back and pulled what he was looking for loose. A single business card.

Daniel Worster. Former colleague of Yannick Duclos' at BH, and the closest thing he had to a friend.

"Why are you showing me this?" I asked, my voice rising. "What do you want, Yannick?"

He pressed the card into my chest.

"Take care of my son," he hissed.

"Does he know something?" I said, my voice rising. "Does he know something about all this?"

I could hear sirens, their wail coming in through the open hatch.

Duclos nodded, opened his mouth as if to speak, but only blood came out.

Then his eyes rolled back, going white again.

37

Two days later. As hospitals go, the Royal Brompton wasn't bad, and under better circumstances—that is to say, less life-threatening—I might've even enjoyed visiting hours here. I added my modest bouquet to the sizable collection Ayesha had quickly amassed. She was sitting up in the bed, reading a copy of *Heat*.

"How's your gut?" I asked.

"Not bad. Surgery was a success. I should be out of here in a couple more days. Just keeping me in for, you know, observation."

I sat in the chair across from her. She still had some lunch on her tray.

"How's your headspace?" I asked.

She picked up the remote and flicked on the telly to some talk show.

"I'm bored. Daytime TV has got to be the biggest weapon against unemployment in this country."

I nodded to the magazine. "Never took you for a fan of the celebrity goss."

"Figured if anyone was going to bring me a book, it'd be you," she said. "The flowers are nice, though. Thank you."

"Least I could do," I said. "You're the first person who has ever been shot in my employ."

She smiled a bit at that.

"No shoot 'em ups with Charlie?" she asked.

"Nah. Lotta tail jobs. Guys who are trying to fake injuries or run out on their bills aren't usually packing heat."

"You weren't expecting Duclos to be, either."

I loosened my tie a bit.

"Yeah," I said. "Thanks for showing up."

She muted the TV.

"No problem," she said. "They told me he didn't make it?"

I nodded.

We sat in silence for a moment.

"What'd the cops say?" she asked.

"I'm on my way to talk to them after this."

"Anything about Annie?"

"There might be some movement on that," I said. "But I'll let you know after I talk to Dunsmore."

Her bed rose a bit more with a squeeze of a button.

"I'm going to be out of here soon, you know," she said.

"Yeah? And?"

"So what's next for you? I'm going to need work."

I shifted in my seat.

"Ash," I said. "Take some time off. You've got nothing to prove to anybody. Rest up."

She shook her head.

"That's not for me," she said. "Like I've said: I like to keep in motion."

I looked at all the flowers. The room smelled like mob boss's funeral.

"Hey, you remember last week?" I asked. "At the bench, before we hit the poker room?"

"Yeah?"

"Your guy. The person who was special to you. What happened?"

"I told you. He died."

"In Afghanistan?"

She shook her head again, but slower.

"No. It was after he came back. His name was John. He was visiting his mom. Tower Hamlets. You know it?"

"Yeah. Rough spot."

"Yeah, it is." She smoothed the blanket in front of her. "Anyhow, he went for a drive after. He liked to do that."

The silence returned. She reached for a juice box. I handed it to her, saving her the stretch.

"Car accident," she said. "Head on collision. It was late at night, the other guy apparently dozed off. He'd been drinking. He made it. John didn't." She took a sip. "And that's it."

"I'm sorry," I said. She shrugged.

"You going to put me back to work or what?" she asked.

"Probably. But in a while." I stood to go.

"Thad. Listen to me." She reached for my hand. "I'm fine."

"But maybe I'm not," I said, buttoning my overcoat.

"Be serious."

"I am." I took a breath. "Captain Ayesha Gill, served in Afghanistan in 2012 as a Female Engagement Officer, spending six months of her tour in Forward Operating Base Oullette. Deployed within the Upper Gereshk Valley Anna and tasked with working with the locals in one of the toughest parts of Helmand Province."

"So you have the internet. Well done."

"Also injured in an IED attack that killed six others, including two civilians."

She said nothing, turning away.

"What's the matter?" I asked. "You thought I didn't know the full details?"

"I did *two* tours," she said. "But other than that, great detective work."

I pointed to the flowers. "Lot of people seem to care about you, Ash. Surely one of those bouquets came from someone who is young and maybe not so dumb, if you were looking to, you know, mix it up a bit."

She sucked the last bit of apple juice from the box and reached over for the tray. "Are you giving someone else… *relationship* advice?"

"Nope," I said. "I'm a PI, not an agony aunt. I'm just making some observations."

"What have you deduced?"

I gave her shin a quick pat as I headed out past the foot of her bed,

"Call me in six months. I'll tell you then." I walked out, giving her a quick nod at the door. Her face was a mask. I couldn't tell if she was disappointed, furious or merely resigned. Either way, she was a soldier. She understood chain of command. If she wanted to work, she certainly could—just not for me, not for a while.

169

Charlie was in the hall, just outside, apparently waiting her turn. I almost walked into her.

"Hey," she said. "All right?"

I nodded.

"How is she holding up?"

"Says she's fine. She's a diesel, that's for sure."

"I just swung by to check in," she said. In her hand was a copy of *The New Yorker* and a giant Toblerone.

"She'll be glad to see you coming," I said, nodding to the loot. "She needs better reading material."

"Thanks."

"Look, I gotta go, sorry," I said. "Cops are going to be expecting me. I gotta give a follow-up statement."

"Oh yeah? Didn't they get everything at the scene?"

"Something new has come to light," I said. "I gotta check it out first."

"OK, well, uh…" she rooted in her pocket and pulled something loose. "Here."

She unfolded it. It was a cheque.

"And I suppose that's made out to me for ten thousand pounds?" I asked.

She nodded.

"I know you said you weren't interested, but this is serious," she said.

"I'm not taking your guy's money," I said. "This is non-negotiable."

"It's not his money," she said. "It's mine. It's from my savings. You can pay me back whenever. Just take it. You're going to get mullered by those maniacs."

I shook my head.

"Thank you, but no," I said. "I appreciate the offer, but I'm serious when I say this: I'm not taking your money."

I turned away.

"You're being childish," she said. "You're still mad that I quit, right? Is that it?"

I turned back.

"You think pretty highly of yourself," I said.

"Defense mechanism. It's to balance out how little you

170

clearly think of me."

"Look, I don't have time for this." I glanced at my watch. "I'm running late as it is."

"Then just take the money," she said. "Stop wasting both our efforts and time."

"How's this for saving time?" I asked, turning away. "Good bye."

I headed to the elevator. She followed me to the door as I hit the button.

"Is this because of something else?" she pushed.

I sighed, resisting the urge to repeatedly stab the button in an attempt to summon the car sooner.

"Something else like what?" I asked.

"You know," she said. She wasn't nervous. She was almost defiant. "You and me. Last Christmas."

I faced her.

"No," I said. "No, it's not about last Christmas or any stupid, misplaced pass I may have made. Thank you, though, for bringing that minor humiliation up for discussion." I tuned back away, content to start at the elevator doors, waiting for it to arrive. My phone buzzed.

"Then why? Just tell me. Your stubbornness here is really something, and I've seen you pretty peevish before."

"It's not about the money," I said, checking my texts. "It's not about last Christmas. It's not even about you quitting as soon as you met this Mr. Right."

I paused—then plowed on.

"You were my *friend*, Charlie. You were probably my best friend. I thought we were building something together, this business, this thing *you* asked *me* to be a part of. Remember that? I thought we were in it together. And you jumped ship the first chance you got."

The elevator pinged, doors now opening. I stepped inside, turning to face her.

"I thought you were my partner, Charlie. You thought you were still just a temp."

I waited for her to say something as the doors closed. She didn't. In the years we worked together, I had never seen her without something to say, some wry observation or snappy comeback.

Finally speechless, then. I had never expected to enjoy it so much. It was a cheap thrill, but I took what I could get.

38

I was in a hurry, owing to a quick stop I needed to make before figuring out my next move with Dunsmore and the cops. It was almost 5 o'clock, and so I knew where my next meeting would be. As he had no idea I was coming, I was hoping he wasn't going to break habit.

I shouldn't have worried. Entering the pub, I spotted Worster and his Savile Row-swaddled ass, already propping up the same stool from when we first met.

"Ginger ale, Phillip," I said, sliding in next to him. The young barman nodded.

"Well, well," he said. "You're changing it up."

"Oh, you know. Important to keep people guessing."

"Occupational hazard?" he asked.

"Necessity," I corrected, pulling my drink in, twirling the straw a bit.

He took a deep pull from his own pint, and by the droop of his eyes and the ruddiness of his cheeks it was not his first.

"Nasty bit of business about Yannick," he muttered.

"Yeah. It was pretty rough."

We sat in silence for a moment.

"You hear anything about the boy?" he asked. His voice was a bit shaky.

"Yeah, I did actually," I said. "Turns out Yannick was fastidious to the point of paranoia. He had a big life insurance policy."

"On himself?" He gave his head a short, sharp shake. "No. How's that going to work, with him getting himself killed during the commission of a crime."

"It wasn't on himself," I said, sipping the Canada Dry. "It was on Annie. Big pay out, Massive, actually. That kid is going to be well taken care of."

173

Worster's pint was empty. He raised his arm, but I reached out and gently pulled it back down towards the bar.

He looked at me sidelong, not willing or able to meet my eyes.

I pulled out the folder. The blood stood out quite a bit against the pale blue windowpane check of his suit's wool.

"Jesus," he said. "What is that?"

"Homework," I said. "Yannick gave it to me. Right before he died. Took me a day or so to figure it out, but there it was."

He started to stand. I put my hand on his shoulder, gentle but firm.

"Why don't you let me get you that drink?" I asked, giving Phillip a wave.

The red was long gone from his cheeks when he settled back down.

"Now I'm no expert," I said, opening the folder. "But even to me, it's clear a lot of the stuff that Yannick was doing here over the last few years at your place of employ was pretty intricate. But turns out you guys still had systems in place to track transactions. Banking security programs, basically, so anything over a certain amount or going to flagged countries sets off the alarms."

Two fresh drinks arrived. I took my time twisting my lemon into it.

"So, to get by some of those precautions, someone had to sign off on suspending those programs. In essence, cancelling the service—meaning it's now a free-for-all, at least in terms of money movement." I pulled out a printed e-mail and slid it over.

"That your signature there, Dan, bottom of the scanned document?"

He drank deeply from the still-settling pint. And nodded.

"So I'm guessing you were in on this the whole time, getting a piece. And nobody knew. And because you guys were just so good at your job you were able to hide this little bit of software gamesmanship from any of your masters."

He rubbed his cheeks.

"Nobody even knew we turned it off," he said. "Turns out

people *thinking* it was in place was enough. So we were able to run our stuff on the side."

"So what happened?"

He took another deep sip. "Would've thought you'd have some ideas about that," he said. "Isn't this the part you're actually an expert in?"

My lips twitched. The thinnest of smiles.

"Glad you asked. I think Duclos disappeared without telling you, likely to protect you. You start freaking out—the proverbial golden goose is gone, and suddenly the cash flow starts drying up. First night we met, you said you were rich, just not *that* rich."

He was finally able to meet my eyes. They were dull and bloodshot, but you could see the hate maybe starting to pool around the edges a bit. I held my smile.

"Well, maybe you wanted to be *that* rich. You said so yourself. And now your chance at it has pulled a runner. So you confront Annie Duclos. You guys were friends, so she would've let you in. You lay it out for her, she threatens to blow the whistle on the whole shebang."

I drank some more ginger ale.

"How am I doing so far?"

"Pretty good, I'll admit," he said.

"So you shoot her. Maybe you panic. Hell, maybe you just want to protect yourself and don't want her running to the cops."

Here he blanched, just a bit more.

"Or maybe you're just like everyone else—you really only want one or two things out of life, and you'll do anything you possibly can to make sure those things happen. People are easy, Worster. Once you understand what they really want, you understand them. And what I understand about you is, no one was going to take your toys away."

He took a deep breath through his nose, letting it come out his mouth. He was trying to slow his heart rate.

"It's a good theory," he said. He was keeping calm, trying to find an angle here, something he could grab on to. "But it does make more sense that Yannick simply left the bunker and killed Annie. I mean, he had mental health problems. And didn't I read somewhere that in cases like this it's usually a loved one involved?"

"Yeah, you're right," I said. "It almost always is, especially when guns are involved. But here's the problem with that theory: The camera in Yannick's bunker will show if he left or not."

He took another breath. Deeper, even.

"So I'll guess we'll see which theory holds up," I said, laying a tenner on the bar and giving Phillip a farewell nod. "Have a Friday."

39

I got off the Tube at Finsbury Park, the wind carrying the keening prayers from the nearby mosque through the darkening sky. I had left Dunsmore a voicemail—I was pretty sure she was still angry, so I made sure that my message was short and to the point. Considering what I had said, I had little doubt she'd call back.

In my flat, I laid down on the couch, TV on mute, happy to let the flickering images keep me company as I tried to grab a nap. My Irish friend was nowhere to be seen outside, but tomorrow was the reckoning. Despite Dunsmore, I debated turning my phone off. I wasn't interested in talking to anyone else, nor enduring the temptation to call anyone for help. Charlie had also messaged a couple of times—both texts remained unanswered. I was tired but too restless, so the sleep wasn't coming. My celling wasn't getting any more interesting, so I sat back up and picked at some of the fried chicken takeaway I snagged on the walk home. My door intercom squawked.

"Yes?" I asked into the speaker.

"It's Copta," was all he said. A man not used to hearing no or being kept waiting, I assumed. I buzzed him in.

Copta looked tired, but he was standing straighter, at least. He surveyed my place with only the polite amount of disdain after I waved him inside. He was alone.

"Where's your shadow?" I asked.

"Magnus has the night off," he said. "He and the wife are going out. Something about celebrating their love, I imagine."

"Must be nice."

"I'm sure it is. But it's telling that you and I spending this of all nights alone, isn't it?"

I said nothing, only nodding to the worn easy chair across

from my couch.

"Right," I said. "What's up?"

"I understand the matter of Yannick Duclos has been... resolved."

"That's a helluva phrasing, but yeah. The investigation is over."

"And you found him."

I nodded. "It's likely there's a bit more to come, but I can't say much. Besides, you're a resourceful guy— I'm sure you can get the details before it's in the press."

"You're a resourceful man, too, Grayle. Clever, too."

"For all the good it's done me, yes."

"I meant what I said when we first met. I had heard of you before."

"Yeah? And in which of your endeavours would that be? Real estate or heroin?"

He crossed his legs.

"Does it matter? I hear things," he said. "Some of those things recently have been about you. I also know you're in trouble."

"It doesn't matter, I suppose. But if you came here to flatter me or impress me, you should know I don't get flush too easily. So: what's up?"

He smoothed out the collar of his sweater, a chunky black cable knit, then reached down beside him. He produced a garish gift bag, bright red and covered with sparkly hearts. He handed it over.

"What's this?" I asked.

"Sorry about the packaging," he said. "Only thing they had when I asked for it to be wrapped."

I opened it, clearing away pink tissue paper before pulling loose a heavy wooden box, cherry black with a gleaming silver clasp. I opened it to find a watch—white face, gold bezel, brown leather strap. I looked over the box to find Copta looking at me expectantly.

"Um," I said. "Thank you?"

He smiled patiently.

"That's a Patek Phillipe," he said. "I thought you liked

178

watches?"

"Yeah, but I'm no expert."

"Then I'm happy to educate you," he said. "Swiss made, of course, and world-renowned. Worn by everyone from Queen Elizabeth II to Duke Ellington."

"Ellington?" I asked, glancing at my stack of old vinyl, rife with swing and jazz. "Seriously?"

He nodded.

"Thank you," I said, more sincerely. "But why are you giving me this?"

"You worked to help Annie and her family," he said. "And… you believed me, Mr. Grayle. This is a gesture of appreciation."

I turned the watch over in my hands. It was a stunning piece, to be sure, somehow balanced between being sleekly modern yet classic. But its elegance came off a bit fussy, a bit delicate. As much as I might like Duke Ellington, I couldn't see myself wearing the same watch a queen did.

"If nothing else," Copta said, perhaps sensing my hesitation, "It's an outstanding investment. One of the few pieces with considerable re-sale value."

I felt a slight surge in my chest, something like adrenalized anticipation.

"Oh yeah?" I said. I was happy my voice held steady.

"Absolutely," he said, standing. "All the papers are in the box, Grayle. I'm sure a reputable dealer would be happy to take that off your hands for a handsome sum."

I nodded, all the while resisting the urge to take a look at how much this set Copta back. Instead, I shook his hand.

"There might even be the card for one in the bag somewhere," he added.

Ah.

"Thank you," I said.

"No bother," Copta said, giving my place a last glance at the door. "Keep it, sell it, whichever you prefer." He buttoned his topcoat. "As I'm sure you know, having options is just another way of having peace of mind."

40

Dunsmore had asked me out for coffee the next day, but neither of us was fooled: I was being summoned. We met at St. James's Park, not far from her work, watching the swans in the water. I brought the beverages. She wordlessly accepted hers as we grabbed a bench.

"So," I said. "How's it goin—"

"Worster confessed," she said. "He flipped yesterday. We had him in the room less than ten minutes."

"Well, then. Congrats."

"The sister is taking in Aiden. He'll be moving with her shortly."

"Spain?"

She nodded, sipping from her paper takeaway cup. I waited.

"Hate this time of year," she muttered. "Grey and miserable. Far from any real holidays."

"You might be in the wrong city," I offered.

"I'm not in the advice mood," she said. "Or the joking."

"You're pretty sour for someone who cleared her first homicide."

"Except I didn't," she said. "You did. Isn't that right?"

I leaned forward, clasping my hands in my lap.

"I was just a few minutes ahead," I said. "I enjoyed… certain advantages."

"Like illegally obtained documents, forensic accounting help from people who didn't have to worry about warrants, and, oh, I would wager maybe even some threats and blackmail along the way?"

My turn to sip.

"The case is over," I said. "Take the win."

She stood, walking away. She threw a glance over her shoulder. I followed.

"My...colleagues, they're really enjoying this," she said. "I've been getting all sorts of jokes. Today, someone actually left a toy metal detector at my desk—all the better to find the next bunker, I suppose."

"Kids can be cruel," I said.

"They weren't kidding about your mouth, at least," she countered.

I stopped.

"I'm guessing you didn't get the promotion," I said.

She shoved her hands deep into her coat's pockets, but held her head high.

"No. I didn't."

"So, what then?" I asked. You got me here to declare war? Tell me you're seeking revenge?"

She finished her coffee.

"No," she said. "Not exactly."

"What then?"

Dunsmore took out some more nicotine gum, popping a piece. She offered the pack. I shook my head.

"You smoke?" she asked.

"I quit," I said. "Ways back."

"Oh, good," she said around the wad in her mouth. "The only clean-living PI in all the land."

"You've obviously got something to say," I said. "And so do I. I took a job, and I worked it. I had a lot on the line, too, and a lot to lose. So you might want to get off whatever high horse you think you've earned in our working relationship."

She smiled, but there was little joy in that slender lift of her lips.

"I know you've got a friend somewhere in the Service," she said.

I shrugged, taking in the still water. "Well, I am a people person."

"Well, that's good to hear, because now you and I are going to be friends."

I squared to face her.

"I'm sorry—how's that?"

"I've been thinking it over," she said. We fell back into step.

181

A pair of joggers weaved past us. "You're clearly privy to a lot of info. That Gill girl is effective, too."

"She's on leave for a bit."

"God," she said, already losing patience. "Look, I'm not arguing with you about this. This is what you and I are going to do. You're gonna keep your ear to the seedy ground people like you walk on. You hear anything related to a major crime, particularly homicide, you will get in touch with me ASAP, and no-one else. And if it happens to be a neat case, easy to wrap up, all the better."

"You're making some big assumptions here," I said. "Cases like this one don't happen too often."

"Well, you'll figure it out," she said. "But get me something."

"And if I should decline?"

She pulled her hands loose from the coat, giving them a quick rub. It was chilly by the lake.

"I'd rather make a friend of you than an enemy," she said. "But that doesn't mean I won't."

I ran the options through my head, quickly, Ayesha's earlier warning about Dunsmore's possible vengeance looming in my head. She had been right, of course. Despite it all, the Detective Inspector still had the upper hand.

"If this is what you want, you got it," I said. "Happy to help local law enforcement, of course."

"Good," she said, her voice flat. "I'll be hearing from you soon, then." She turned away, and her posture and pace made it clear our summit was concluded. I sat at another bench. Leaned back. Watched Dunsmore stalk off. Sat a bit longer, watching the city go by.

41

That Valentine's Day text had been from my old friend Sarah, whose aspiring journalist son Jeremy had been somewhat insistent about career day. She happily informed me her son attended St. Ann's. Sighing inwardly, I told her I wouldn't need directions.

When she called, I had been resting up after getting Quigley and his band of merry legbreakers their cash following the sale of the watch, flush with relief and feeling I deserved a distraction. Agreeing to speak to his class now found me sitting in front of a roomful of feet-shuffling, uniformed Year Tens, the elite-yet-disaffected of our youth. I was next to a big-bellied firefighter and a nervous-looking veterinarian.

"You all right?" I asked the vet as we shook hands. Damp palms.

He nodded. "Not much of a speaker. Better with pets, I guess."

"Kids love animals," I said, trying to be reassuring.

"Not when they find out part of my job is putting them down," he said.

"Maybe don't open with that," I said, standing to take their questions. "Don't worry. I'll tank a little bit, lower their expectations."

Miss Williams, the teacher, was a slim young woman whose eagerness seemed well-matched to her sunny smile. She quickly introduced me as Jeremy's guest. She ushered me to the front of the class, explaining she imagined part of my job was to help the police.

"Or stay out of their way," I said. I gave the class a half-wave. "Hey."

They stared at me blankly. A lone cough was half-suppressed from the back.

"So. Um." I rifled through my pockets, pulling loose a sheet with some notes on it. I was clearly out of practice being in front of a classroom.

"Do you have a gun?" a ruddy faced girl in the front asked.

I shook my head. "No, I'm not really a fan. Plus, they are super illegal here."

"Where are you from?" she quickly followed up, my accent giving me away.

"Seattle. United States. Go Mariners."

"Have you ever shot anyone, though?" someone else called out.

I looked at the teacher. She shrugged, although her smile had dimmed slightly.

I shook my head once again.

"No, I haven't," I said. "Well, not yet, anyways."

The vet laughed. No one else did.

"Do you go through people's garbage?" someone else called out.

"Yeah, sometimes," I said. "People throw out all sorts of stuff that they forget can get them in trouble."

"Like what?"

"Well, uh, forged cheques, sometimes. Credit card bills with stuff on 'em people shouldn't be buying. E-mail hard copies with stuff they shouldn't say. You know, love letters to the wrong people…" My voice trailed a little bit as I could feel my throat tightening. I saw Jeremy shifting in his seat.

"My mom hired a PI," another kid called out. "She found out my dad had another family."

"OK," Miss Williams said. "Let's thank our guest—"

"I used to do that work," I said. "But not any more. I mainly work for insurance companies now and other folks who need background work done."

"Do you make a lot of money?"

"Well, I'm not rich," I said. "But I'm my own boss. So I don't often do anything I don't want to do."

"That's cool," one of them said, and a slight murmur spread through the group.

A tentative knock on the door interrupted. Some younger

students filed in, Miss Williams explaining that they were given the chance to see some of the senior class's presentations.

Aiden stood in the back, apart from his classmates who excitedly grabbed seats next to the big kids. He was stiff, his arms crossed, eyes downcast.

"What was your last case like?" the ruddy faced girl called out.

Aiden looked up.

I looked over at Miss Williams, hoping she was going to try and wrap this up again, but she had sat back at her desk, looking at me attentively.

"Um," I said. "You know, some cases you can't talk about. Confidentiality."

"Have you ever seen a dead body?" another kid quickly followed up. They were keen now, sensing I was holding back.

Aiden and I made eye contact.

The room patiently awaited my answer.

I scratched my chin.

Aiden held my gaze.

Take care of yourself, kid was all I could hope he read in my eyes.

"You know what?" I said. "It's a pretty boring job. You guys watch a bit too much telly."

"Could I be a PI?" another kid called out, a boy of about 15 and already built like a diesel engine, his collar straining at his pocked neck.

Aiden's eyes were tired, red. He looked away.

"Sure," I said, gathering my coat to leave and nodding to Miss Williams. "Why not? They'll pretty much let anyone do it."

The vet nodded good-bye. I walked out, careful in closing the door behind me.

Epilogue

It was not yet 4 o'clock and so Bowering's place was relatively empty, and certainly quiet, save for the meek beeps from the decades-old fruit machine tucked away in the back. I pulled up to the bar.

"Well, well," he said. "Look who's still in one piece."

I shrugged, trying to hide the low-glow of joy inside me that persisted, despite everything else that had happened the last few days.

I checked my phone again. Charlie's message had spilled over into a longer e-mail. She was disappointed with how things had been left and she wanted to have a chance to talk. I couldn't tell if she expected an apology or not. I didn't know if I would be willing to give it, either.

Bowering presented me with a pint of cola.

"No diet stuff for you today," he said. "After a brush with death, treat yourself to some actual sugar."

I smiled my thanks and took a sip. He lingered.

"What's up?" I asked.

He scratched his chin. "Remember that project we talked about a ways back, the one I got you to check the kid out for suitability?"

I nodded.

"Well, the long and the short of it this: We are picking up debts from other, ah, lenders at a cut price and them collecting them for ourselves."

"How does that work?" I asked, amused. "Like a collections agency?"

"Something like that," he said, wiping down the bar. "Some guys disappear, and it's just not cost efficient for the lender to try and track them all over Europe, or hell, the world. So we pick up the sheet for pennies on the pound and try to collect if and when the opportunity presents itself."

I considered this entrepreneurial turn.

"Not bad," I admitted. "Your idea?"

Bowering nodded.

"You put the kid, Raynott, on it?"

"Nah. You guys were right. He's too nice."

"Well, it's a good manager who recognizes both his team member's talents and limitations," I said, raising my glass.

"Thanks," he said, taking my light snark in stride. "So far, it's been a pretty good side business for us."

"Well, continued success with it," I said, standing. I laid a few quid on the bar. He scooped it up and dropped it in the register before returning.

"No change," I said.

"No, no," he said. He laid out a piece of paper. "This is someone who came to our attention. Thought you might be interested."

I sat back down, unfolding the slip and taking a look at the name.

"That's your boy, isn't it?" Bowering asked. "Guy who left you holding a pretty big bag?"

There it was, in neat black block letters. Taylor Brock and his current address, somewhere in darkest Birmingham. Hell, they even had his e-mail and mobile number.

"Bag big enough for ten thousand pounds, yeah," I said. My stomach was already in a slow roll. "How'd you get this?"

"I have a few associates up north," he said. "Obviously, the debt has been settled, thanks to you, so there's no job there for us anymore."

I stared at the paper for what was beginning to feel like a long time.

"Of course, that doesn't mean someone else wouldn't want to swing by," he said. "You know, just drop in. Have a chat, like."

Another punter came in and headed to the far end of the bar, calling out for a pint of Stella. Bowering drifted to the taps.

I picked up the paper, giving it a final once-over. Neatly folding it, I slipped it into my jacket, careful to button the inside pocket.

"How we doing?" Bowering asked. "Another Coke?"

My phone buzzed one more time. I glanced down.

Charlie. Again.

I shook my head.

"Nah," I said. I shifted on the stool, loosening my tie. I looked over Bowering's shoulder and pointed to the top shelf.

"What kind of whiskey you got?" I asked.

Fantastic Books
Great Authors

CROOKED
CAT

Meet our authors and discover
our exciting range:

- Gripping Thrillers
- Cosy Mysteries
- Romantic Chick-Lit
- Fascinating Historicals
- Exciting Fantasy
- Young Adult and Children's
  Adventures
- Non-Fiction

Made in the USA
Middletown, DE
23 June 2019